/

root

Also by Adam Engel

Topiary, 2009

I Hope My Corpse Gives You the Plague, 2010

Cella Fantastick, 2011

All by Oliver Arts & Open Press

For the Free Software Foundation: GNU-Linux: and Richard Stallman:

In memory of Barbara Mor:

Forever dreaming Spring.

ISBN: 9780988334373
Library of Congress Control Number: 2016908480

The Oliver Arts & Open Press, LLC
2578 Broadway, Suite #102
New York, NY 10025
www.oliveropenpress.com

/

root

Adam Engel

THE OLIVER ARTS & OPEN PRESS

The Information Systems Integration Structure (ISIS) operating system was originally conceived by a bored System Administrator in 1997. It is not related to any other "ISIS" — real or imagined.

"Any one user — with or without privileged access — surrounded by an organized properly paralleled and mirrored hierarchy of processors: terminals: servers: gadgets: do-dads: flub-dubs: whirly-gigs and protocols particular to the OS (under euphemistic guise of Interface between the user and The System) will be compelled to speak — if only to himself — the language of ISIS."

— /

"Time happened: and there was no escape: not even to the Word."

— **Scrivener**

Information System's Integration Structure (ISIS)

In ISIS many stories beneath the Law: root (/) administered the System.

1.

All screens and monitors are bi-directional. Users peering at familiar faces on Social Network sites — "friends" seldom encountered in person — are typically shocked and humiliated (prophylactic Mickey Finn brewed by psychiatrists in Human Resources to thwart litigious notions re: "invasion of privacy" via 24/7 surveillance) to receive punitive messages regarding "improper use of company time and property" from the unseen faces whose eyes watch everything everywhere: always.

2.

Screens connected to disc-less dumb-terminals at user-level default to the Company Logo when unattended for three minutes: a lascivious-but-tasteful rendering of a woman — nude of course — offers the user an iridescent fig.

2.1.

The woman whispers "Eat my fig" or the name of the current user followed by the Company slogan: "Knowledge is dangerous…"

3.

Monitors assigned to machines/users of more privileged access are permitted display variations on the prescribed theme — within limits proscribed by official Company guidelines. For instance: the monitors of 4-Sector default to the same nude woman: however: in 4-Sector's version a glossy-black serpent en-folds Fig-Woman while she slithers snake-like-seductive up-down-and-around her dance-pole.

3.1.

In 4-Sector's hyper-realistic depiction Fig-Woman extends her vulva-lipped fruit and whispers "Eat *Boobeleh!*"

3.1.1.

4-Sector's rendition is over-solicitous: tenderly sly: not quite professional. But within official guidelines — as written.

3.1.1.2.

Company guidelines may be subject to revision. Use of slang and non-standard language have yet to be defined: standardized: submitted for Official Review.

3.1.2.

In custom-configured versions of the animation the name of the user is spoken aloud — usually restricted to those with access-privilege to configure animations as well as permission to operate the software required for such unofficial digi-doodling.

3.1.2.1.

The stark Fig-Woman re-appears upon user log-off to utter a helpful thought or maxim — typically the Default Loop. When illegally customized she mouths more suggestive — possibly sardonic: nasty: even seditious — statements.

3.1.2.2.

Whatever certain Cowboy-Coders of the Third-LAN punch into her thin silicone heart.

4.

Information System's Integration Structure (ISIS): The Company's Operating System (OS).

5.

IMG (Information Management Graphics): the graphic user interface (GUI) of ISIS.

6.

The ISIS Operating System is mind of The Company: the Database its memory: the Intra-Net its voice.

7.

The Network is Voice of All.

8.

Data flows like a river fighting wind. Input. Output. Redirection (for those with guts to blow upstream).

9.

Some Expert Professionals would like to change the river's course.

9.1.

They hesitate.

10.

All Executive communication in ISIS is encrypted at the highest high-gear baddest-ass levels of mathematical subterfuge commercially available — or on the black-market if push comes shove: as it always does.

11.

Acknowledgement that ISIS or any other aspect of The Network is a soul-sucking death-loop iterating bad Karma might conceivably provoke Spontaneous Redirection.

12.

Any one user — with or without privileged access — surrounded by an organized properly paralleled and mirrored hierarchy of processors: terminals: servers: gadgets: do-dads: flub-dubs: whirly-gigs and protocols particular to the OS (under euphemistic guise of Interface between the user and The System) will be compelled to speak — if only to himself — the language of ISIS.

13.

Positioned as an ever-threatening secret network The Third LAN exists to exist. They might serve as eye of counter-snoop: but only to see what they can see. Each of these alleged Coder-Clusters or Cyber-Cells — separated by oceans and continents — are expected to maintain access to and communication with all other cells. They can create a free network within The Network's audio-visual extravaganza: but nobody knows what each node is thinking: especially nodes comprised of humans. Why should one trust the Third LAN any more or less than one would trust The Powers of Organized Network (POON)?

13.1.

In truth: the Third LAN with its odd and various hackers — spanning all time-zones: committed to attack attack attack — might perhaps do some small damage to the Network if not actually bring the beast down (no one actually believes the Network can be stopped: merely diverted: on occasion).

13.2.

The obvious question: who but Those Who Know know whether the Third LAN is not itself the brain-child of cunning Networked minds (that is: Those Who Know?)

14.

It wasn't my fault. Things happened slow. At first. I caught on quick. By age sixteen I could no longer relate to the majority of my peers. Their ossification had begun. The deeper I delve (beyond my will at this point) into The System: the more untamed data I acquire: the greater grows the distance between myself and those I've loved.

14.1.

I have loved. I'm almost certain.

15.

Occasionally Sudden System Data-blasts (SSD's) occur. Unexpected: at first. Now expected: though Algorithms of Prediction (ALGOP) are as faulty as projections of an earthquake's encore: and just as unpredictable. These SSD's are the more-or-less-expected vomiting of indigestible data: the System expunging hairball bits of data from itself: a periodic purging preparatory to Self-renewal.

16.

When / becomes Superuser he wields absolute power over ISIS: however: it is the machine — guardian-keeper of itself — to whom / must abjectly and daily submit alpha-numeric pass-code petitions for entry.

17.

WIT (Word Interchange Terminal): the text-command-manipulation terminal restricted to System Administrators (SysAdmins) such as / for script-writing: system maintenance: and secure communication with and within ISIS.

17.1.

WIT is /'s shell-within-his-shell within his box within his cubicle behind the firewall down in the sub-basement offices of /'s creator and keeper: Administrative Systems Security (ASS) of the Central Year-One Systems Technology (CYST) division of The Company.

17.1.1.

WIT is /'s link to others of his kind: those whose Permission Access Yield (PAY) quotients the typical user could hardly conceive of much less aspire to.

18.

/ had a name: it was almost certainly printed on his ASS card and Company ID.

18.1.

/'s personal data was linked — secretly and obliquely — to dummy accounts / had created to administer tests and spoofs disguised as common users.

18.1.1.

/ began and ended each day logged-in as Superuser: hands eyes and wet-ware intelligence of the System: anonymous.

18.1.2.

High Access Tactical (HAT) clearance-level is restricted to a tiny group of essential operators such as /. Passwords change weekly as do encryption keys. All sessions are closed but monitored.

18.1.3.

Because after all: any clown in a HAT can become almighty Superuser. And — given the chance — will.

18.1.4.

When security-holes dilate events slink through. Hence: The System runs on Hypothetical Alert (HA) — always.

19.

As System Administrator / is tasked with overseeing CYST's internal and external connections.

20.

/ was not in the habit of using IMG (Information Management Graphics). Like most essential Administrators he relied exclusively on command-line text editors: but unlike certain Administrators to whom one text-editor was the same as any other / always preferred to communicate with WIT.

21.

/'s message of the day to /: "I have knowledge: why aren't I dangerous?"

22.

/'s updated Message of the Day to /: "Be dangerous."

23.

/ labored years to learn and master protocols of ISIS: where will it all go?

23.1.

Will /'s wet-ware be scheduled for replication and back-up before he dies?

23.2.

Will / attain transcendence upon uploading his wet-ware contents to The Cloud?

23.3.

If so: who might know *when* this is to occur — approximately?

24.

"ISIS is the book I've always wanted to write but cannot it's too big tremendous too complex I'm just a man a little man with limited options: what else can I do? I must *read* her" quoth /.

25.

There is no citizenry no public: no small cabals of literate like-minded technorati. There's only what's Out There on the Networked City/Prison/Detention-camp planner's surveillance wet dream. Hecatombs of monad flicker in and out of Networked Space-Time-Continuous. Log-on-log-off unpredictable as quanta: traceable as fingerprints.

26.

A Primal Executive of The Company — reclining deep: feet-crossed-on-desk: his office many stories above earth — phoned / with the cheerful urgency of Someone In Charge:

Is the Network broken? I'm not certain but I think I broke the Network: the mail and Net-View parts at any rate. I pressed a button or some-such-thing-a-ma-jig I shouldn't have been fiddling with. Lesson learned. You know: like they say: "whaddya gonna do?" Right? *Mea Culpa.* Anyway: think you can fix this by noon? I have a conference scheduled: a Networked conference. It would be reasonable to assume that this meeting among powerful but distant colleagues will not occur without a functioning Network: yes? Fix it.

27.

Processors of input-output. Error.

28.

I'm not at all angry: which really pisses me off.

29.

The Network lode of fear duplicity and paranoia inspires ignorant users to cry "Breech of trust!" Such users do not understand Systems Security (SS). Data Ubiquity Protocols of Engagement (DUPE) and Standard Administration Procedure (SAP) assume conventions of breech not trust — tactical first-strike options are always on the table.

30.

Eighty-hour-a-week battle plan.

31.

Everyone likes pets and kids. All little dogs boys and girls have their job responsibilities and work-ethic in which duty ranks second only to the ardor with which it is performed.

31.1.

Dogs and children instinctively fax progress reports — complete with cover-memos — to their superiors.

31.1.1.

Dogs and children understand that a cliché such as "The Boss wants what the Boss wants" is itself a chunk of arcana whose true meaning is revealed only to Those Who Know.

31.1.2.

Dogs and children understand that the so-called trope or cliché is itself hard-coded into The System: *so they do not fuck with it.*

32.

The Network is hardly the end of individual consciousness — that went long-ago: it is the killing-blow: *the coup-de-grace.*

32.1.

Hints of dementia pop up here and there among the millions of Net-sites not under full jurisdiction of Network Wellness Syndicate (NEWSYN) — a voluntary non-profit social service conglomerate with various Flag-ship Sites providing common users with a customizable template of relatively expansive data-estate (10 gigs) free-of-charge.

32.1.1.

In exchange for this free-of-charge service NEWSYN acquires full access to all of the users' files and information via a back-door — encrypted in utmost secrecy under aegis and authority of NEWSYN. "I'm your back-door Man-ager" assures the NEWSYN community outreach tag.

32.1.2.

NEWSYN knows what you like. They know what you hate. They know if you've been naughty or nice. If the former you'll know too: soon enough.

33.

Money Law Architecture birthed on paper after gestation — long or short according to budget — in Womb of Mind (WOM). All is fiction in this simulacrum of an illusion of a make-believe world. But / has heard that once there had been others: extinct examples of natural life: long long ago.

33.1.

This natural life was hard as all life was and is: but according to legend this alleged life was neither humiliating-ridiculous nor despicable: incredible though this might seem (extinct regardless: so *fuhgeddaboudit*: ain't happening).

33.1.1.

This could be more mere talk. But there appears to be much corroborating evidence found at archaeological digs under the layers of fossil turd and broken pottery that conceal the everyday-life of History like redacted documents conceal what you shouldn't know because it's *nonna yer damned beeswax*.

33.1.2.

Hidden and forgotten places stacked with glyptic clues: outright statements in cuneiform-hieroglyph-rune: and plain-old marks on walls. Also: cryptic (i.e. not deciphered — yet) messages on artifacts and stones.

34.

Information is the liquid Currency of ISIS and Data Storage its gold standard.

35.

The Company is good for the economy.

36.

Like: duh.

37.

Really I'm just a television repair man.

38.

It all grows so complex — and boring. Protocols. Encryption. Compatibility of hard-ware/software under proprietary ownership and licensed manufacture. Metaphors. Information Packets. Does an information packet really exist the way a mango or a can of soup exists? / had never actually seen an information packet other than as illustrations depicted in fat textbooks during Universal Systems Environment Resource (USER) training.

38.1.

Graphs and diagrams for analysis: evaluation: research: depict the information packet from New-IMG perspectives of deep-concept visualization.

39.

Sequence switch-on switch-off electric signal one-zero. Or zero-one. Positive and negative. Yin-Yang. Abstract dualities hypothesized: systematized: addressed.

39.1.

Evolution of Imagine from crude clay tablets to multifarious multi-dimensional IMG Metaphorical-Environments (IM-ME) and productivity suites.

40.

The common user — regardless of proficiency in this or that word-processing date-and-appointment-scheduling or image-manipulation software — knows as little of the System in which his/her data lives moves and interacts with other data as the average driver knows auto mechanics or couch-potato the physics of television transmission.

40.1.

/ knows little about cars and televisions and cares even less. He surrendered his driver's license at age 23 and quit television cold-turkey at 20 because he did not know how cars or televisions worked and had no interest in learning: truly he didn't want to know.

41.

Packets of data delicate as eggs: simile's abstraction.

42.

You do not write words on a word processor the way we think of writing with a pen or type-writer. You deposit quick-as-thought thoughts silently on ultra-sensitive touch-pads keyboards screens. Once deposited these thoughts remain in system storage (occasionally accruing interest — rarely: no-one's ever actually interested but the Department of Systems Security (DOSS)) until released by one with appropriate expertise and access: such as the SysAdmin.

42.1.

Nebulous mind-stuff reified. Immediate lines on-screen styled in whatever font you choose from the System's woof of symbiotic parameters protocols paradigms and procedures for printing (assuming printer access-privilege — or you've got problems: Bud!).

42.2

Thoughts can be erased or withdrawn until made manifest on paper.

42.3.

If the printer doesn't work or you do not have access-permission your thoughts will continue to exist on the local and/or System drive like souls in purgatory: and you better have backed them up to a personal storage-device lest a bored-to-the-point-of-deviance SysAdmin such as / decide to exercise full control over ISIS and all its works ("control" relative to his finite wet-ware self) and smoke your stuff.

42.4.

Zip-it. Zap-it. Waste it. Blast-it. Poof. Gone. "See you in /dev/null."

43.

There's money to be made.

44.

When you die you will no longer be able to log on to the Network.

44.1

When you die you may receive email: but you may not answer it.

45.

The Network contains all the information in existence: but very little wisdom.

46.

The paragraph is the largest chunk of integrated data the Infocracy can manage.

46.1

No room in Networked Space-Time-Continuous for concepts requiring more than a paragraph of text to explain or comprehend whatever-the-hell one might be saying or trying to say.

46.2.

Emily Dickinson and Arthur Rimbaud will be the poet-laureates of Networked Infocracy.

47.

Infocratic sentences are semiotic units self-contained.

47.1.

An Infocratic sentence must exist within the boundaries and protocols of its Standardized Language of Origin (SLO).

48.2.

The Infocratic sentence must be object-oriented and function within language-specific protocols of class: hierarchy: inheritance: and parental lineage from origin Ur-Self to present and future descendant objects.

49.

The Acronym is the fundamental linguistic unit — a kind of zip-gun signifier — for Standard Infocratic Discourse (SID).

49.1.

For instance: IOPS is an acronym for I/O per second: which is itself an acronym for input/output. Per second.

50.

Spiraling to labyrinth...

51.

Like most primary objects the acronym will become parent to smaller units of information: many of which themselves will be comprised of acronyms.

51.1.

Much as the trustees on the Company's Board of Trustees are not actual persons but other companies: each Trustee-unit votes by proxy for whatever directive had been decided well in advance by its own Russian-doll Boards of Executives: Shareholders: Trustees.

52.

Software not hardware is the mind-stuff of Infoconomy.

52.1.

But as They (you know: Them) say: "Bound mind bound body."

53.

Software accelerates liquidity-and-transfer of information: but information *qua* information (mirrored and secured) is the Infocracy's gold-standard bulwarking and securing reproducible symbolic cash pointers referencing said information with accuracy-degree levels that vary with fluctuation of real value.

53.1.

Some folks — particularly Those Who Own Stuff — take all this information-exchange and symbolic-pointers-to-value rigmarole very very seriously.

54.

The Infocracy is hierarchical.

54.1.

Gee: ya think?

55.

The Infocracy is a hierarchy of Those Who Know: Those Who Sell: and those Who Know and Sell.

56.

The Infocracy will feed off entropy of the masses and other less potent (that is: organized) entities.

57.

The Infocracy itself is comprised of relatively few persons — corporate: government: other — but many complicated systems.

58.

The Network exists for political: social: economic and intellectual enrichment of Infocracy.

59.

The masses will support Infocracy with credit debt and wide-spread — near total — inability or refusal to detect patterns.

60.

The much-ballyhooed replacement of mortal History with transcendent Systems may cause side-effects. Such as the morbid dementia-unto-catatonia most users develop in allergic reaction to relentless wave-form shivers of anxiety-depression: fear-despair: and other pathologies epistemologically: ontologically: and for-damned-shit-sure-bulls-eye-dead-on related to their ridiculous boring harried lives.

60.1

As history loses relevance so too do fictions and mythologies that evolved from the love of life and the pathos of death.

61.

Beware the day-to-day: indoctrination methods are more subtle and acute during Clock-Routine Time than the Prime-Time Network-channel   surf-at-home zip-zap-zow-bing-blap high-powered electronic (or-nuclear — depending upon The Client's preference: whatever-it-takes man!) hard-sell.

61.1

There's new more better stuff — at least better than the stuff you got now cause it's new — so buy it ass-hole!

61.2.

Get off the damned couch and accumulate: *obtain* for god-sake.

62.

"Dis?" When was / ever "enchanted?"

63.

All new fictions that are permitted to exist will mirror our bleak realities decked-out-dolled-up in silicon drag and *cyber-haute couture.*

64.

ISIS is full of words. In his capacity as SysAdmin / is full of ISIS.

64.1.

Is there a world inside /?

64.2.

Or is the world inside /?

65.

Also includes these fine plug-ins: Data-Scorch: Counterfeit:
and an upgraded release of Cyanide — the deep-core kill-
switch ever-so-handy in extreme emergencies.

66.

/:

All those imported greens: shrubs: tubers: exotic fruit-things and animal parts tastefully displayed in the cafeteria. What system defines their coming to the pricey Company buffet? What process determines their arrival? There are systems beyond the System: Horatio: not dreamed of in your TV Guide.

67.

Multi-Tasknician:

Artists and "creatives" like the IMG-only guys up in Public Communications are reputedly insane.

71.

Scrivener:

Clobber the squab-ash: deflower the fuss-budget: scarify blister fulminate fustigate blight blast nip.

72.

Net-Ma'am:

Everything is fiction. Money: law: architecture. Everything on screens or paper born of inspiration-spark or gradual gestation within Womb of Mind (WOM).

73.

/:

Really I'm just a television repair-man: wearing a stupid tie. And carrying a loop of alpha-numeric code keys to hush-hush secret virtual rooms: raw-data mines: trap-doors: back-doors: and other highly Secured and Surveyed (Sec-N-Surv) stuff. Like a prison guard: who repairs TVs.

74.

Systems Analyst:

The Network is the organizational model of Infoconomy. Now all the people can have two jobs and manufacture children who will one day work 70-80 hour weeks to keep the Network running faster and more efficiently than Mom and Dad could ever have dreamed — or cared to imagine.

75.

Scrivener:

The Network is cold and hard as a stiletto: lifeless: only as nasty as the Entities who wield it.

76.

/:

If people exist for the Network would it be bad if they did not exist at all?

77.

Net-Ma'am:

Systems are self-regulating. Like vaginas.   So I've heard. Maybe I read it somewhere.

78.

/:

A cigar is real: a Network protocol is not. Just my two cents.

79.

Desktop-Memo Applet:

Deposit thoughts interest align currency socket: format.

80.

Desktop-Memo Applet Upgrade:

You snooze you lose. Outta here dude: you've got bugs.

81.

Cowboy-Coder:

How does that old saw go? Something like: "You can't wreck the Master's house without authorized government-safety-approved power-tools" or whatever? Always annoyed me. You can wreck the Master's house with any fucking tools you want. Or you can at least try. What you most certainly *cannot* do is serve the Master a summons printed for "the Court" he owns on the Master's own damned printing press. You know: like: man?

82.

/:

On Line Transaction Processing (OLTP).

83.

Systems Analyst:

Mean Cycle Between Failure (MCBF).

84.

Scrivener:

Energy. All life forms seek unlimited supplies of energy. What the fuck does that mean? What am I talking about? What am I thinking? I'm sitting in front of a screen: typing words that probably should not exist — to the extent they do exist (I didn't press "Print" yet). The screen creates an alpha-numeric simulacrum of talk. Talk. Worthless. Blip. Touch of a button. Gone. Poof. Blown away. Disintegration of a chat.

85.

Cowboy-Coder:

A fart in the wind of existence...

86.

/:

Management Information Broker (MIB).

87.

Systems Analyst:

Simple Network Management Protocol (SNMP).

88.

/:

Random Arrays of Individual Deployment (RAID).

89.

Systems Analyst:

Annualized Failure Rate (AFR).

90.

Primal Partner of the Company:

In today's economy it pays to to shut up and do as you're told. We don't want no trouble: see?

90.1.

Systems Analyst:

Think parity. Bits and bytes reserved in segments. Data spreads wide-far: if you lose one drive — real or virtual — the others have all or most of the information necessary to rebuild it. This is how The Company solidifies its human resource base. Everyone specializes in his/her area of expertise but retains a modicum of knowledge in another area. Should an employee with enough data exposure to be valuable disappear he/she can be rebuilt from wet-ware iterations of even a fresh recruit or intern via immersion-training among employees briefed to retain parallel data sequences.

90.2.

Multi-Tasknician:

Configure: make: install. What could be simpler?

91.

/:

Striping. Knowledge is "chunked" and shared among a series of employees. Hence any one unit is quick-easily accessed: but all rely on others. You need them all for the full picture. But once the picture's complete: saved: replicated: the aforementioned employees can get gone — according to mood whim and alibi of Management.

92.

Systems Analyst:

Mirroring. Employees *abcd* are fed the same data as employees 1234. Should one employee crash another will immediately replace him.

92.1.

Systems Analyst:

Requisite knowledge-base and parallel skill-sets are assumed.

92.2.

Systems Analyst:

However: this can cost money.

92.3

/:

Touché.

93.

Primal Partner of The Company:

Standardization. To establish relevance: market-value: mystique. Else: nothing means anything at all.

94.

Scrivener:

The Digital Age began many eons ago with Power's reduction of complex relationships (human-human: not human-machine) to the rock-solid dialectic of Yes-or-No.

94.1.

Net-Ma'am:

Master Servers and their Slaves: a complex relationship?

94.2.

Graphic-Design-Gal:

Company policy for obtaining knowledge: pain. Regardless of sweat: blood: tears. Despair of sentience.

94.3.

Scrivener:

I suppose if one must serve who better to serve than the Server?

95.

Systems Analyst:

Listen to the reliability specs. Ten thousand hours MTBF per standard employee.

96.

Multi-Tasknician:

Storage backup data loss = lost time storage data no back-up.

97.

/:

Data is an impartial mediator of human experience. Living entities programmed the System to capture moments lived: duplicated: and arranged according to algorithms of random iteration only god or ISIS could know.

97.1.

Cowboy-Coder:

Or the "living entities" themselves. They might know an algorithm or two…

98.

Scrivener:

Life as Art in the Age of Digital Mass Re-production.

98.1.

Cowboy-Multi-Tasknician:

Death in the binary-octa-hexa-decimal afternoon.

99.

Net-Ma'am:

The duplicate is not the Life. In Data we find (that is: the System finds) intimate details of lives: medical and psychiatric records: backgrounds of criminal or ungrateful acts: financial histories. Someone defaults on a loan: receives grim letters in Bank-or-Government seal — and trembles.

99.1.

Net-Ma'am:

This is the record of that trembling.

100.

Multi-Tasknician:

Sealed away from relevance: while outside the tabloids cry "we was robbed" — but blame it on keepers and maintainers of the System: not the System itself.

101.

/:

Regular performance-testing is crucial.

101.1.

Scrivener:

Test crucial what?

101.2.

/:

Crucial ISIS. The System. Imagine an individual lost in the System. Completely alone. But still ridiculous-hungry to be relevant: to be important: to have value: some toenail crescent of control over... something. What could this individual — wandering electric catacombs — possibly do but dream revenge? Hence-thus-and-so-forth: it is crucial to simulate replicate and solve such situations as the ISIS mish-mash of Dispassionate Over-flow Access (DOA) iterations might conceivably ignite.

102.

Systems Analyst:

Remote Procedure Call (RPC).

103.

/:

CERT. CERN. NCSA.

104.

Multi-Tasknician:

In the city where I studied for and received my degree in Formal Languages (Procedural: Functional: Object-oriented) French fries accompanied every dish: even salad. All sandwiches side-plates entrées on lunch and dinner menus everywhere featured a choice of three or more cheese toppings: melted — unless otherwise requested via explicit instruction to the wait-staff.

105.

Cowboy-Coder:

People made stuff. With their minds and hands. Once. Things they could use. Or just look at or listen to cause it was pretty. But then machines factories assembly-line junk. No shit the poor bastards trapped inside the machines felt "alienated." Disjointed. Shattered. Smashed.

106.

Net-Ma'am:

Morning cigarette: coffee: radio-talk-news. Upstream-struggle to The Job.

107.

Scrivener:

People in front of screens buying and selling numbers symbolic of real or arbitrary "value" of XY amount of goods and services. The symbolic structure ceases to exist — temporarily — when the machine is unplugged: however: the goods and services may or may not exist or cease to exist independent of symbolic representation: they may or may not have ever existed at all.

108.

Multi-Tasknician:

Wary of both Believe-It-or-Not and Designed-For-Your-Convenience I learned the Machine and cultivated mastery of Process-Language (PLAN): in order to tune-in. I've no idea how long it will take me to figure a way out. Rest of my life? This whole package — systems networks languages protocols — is one big fucking shape-shifting fractal that disappears at 11:59 PM and reappears promptly — upgraded and remodeled — at midnight.

109.

/:

Audio-graphic-video-narratives with animation squeaky sounds and pop-up road-sign help-text.

110.

Primal Partner of the Company:

They're not *supposed* to be your friends: they're the Competition.

111.

Scrivener:

Ever go into a bookstore open a new book just stand there and smell it?

111.1.

Net-Ma'am:

I remember books.

112.

Graphic-Design-Gal:

What gives you pleasure? What can you touch?

113.

/:

I'd like to touch that Company Logo. Fig-Woman. She wants to be touched. By Superuser. I know she does: she wants to be probed by /. But you can't be touched over the network. Connected: but not touched. Particularly if the person you wish to touch is a 3D painting of a model hired from an agency with no connection to the Company in any damaging: incriminating: or defamatory fashion.

114.

Scrivener:

Lost in the folds of Networked time…

115.

/:

Lost in the folds of Fig-Woman's labia...

116.

Graphic-Design-Gal:

Cowboy-up Superuser.

116.1.

Net-Ma'am:

Yeah. Women present.

116.2.

/:

Of course. Your text-talk comes through in distinctly feminine font. You will please pardon me: Mademoiselle Net-Ma'am.

116.3.

Net-Ma'am:

Consider yourself redeemed. Voucher can be downloaded with easy one-time entry of account number pass-code valid credit card and whatever other information Security deems necessary to procedures of identity verification and clearance or for shits-and-giggles.

117.

Scrivener:

We'll be all be touched soon enough. By the Network. Text manipulation programs like Word-Up are so connected to everything and all you can't write a private memo to your own damned self without certain Someones getting a first look-see.

118.

Net-Ma'am:

When They lower the big fluffy pillow to smother us we will not scream.

119.

Cowboy-Coder:

The Network is a poison spider. Constant signals constantly probing. Perpetual bombardment. Harassment. Aggression. Kill the fucker. Bring it down.

120.

/:

Bring down the Network? But then / will be alone in his cubicle overseeing the three thousand some-odd nodes comprising The Company Database and Intra-Net: alone with racks and racks of System Back-up and RAID drives shoring The Company's Data against ruin.

121.

Scrivener:

Random Assaults of Information Discharge. So much energy. Tremendous cooling systems. The Company sucks energy from the City's sucking of the world. Dark Clouds over-head.

121.1.

Cowboy-Coder:

The Clouds move ceaselessly impossible to pin.

120.2.

/

Every Cloud its silver server — distant. For just-in-case.

121.3.

Systems Analyst:

Backup backup. Clouds prevent forest fires. The Tree of Knowledge must not burn.

122.

/:

I am a television repair man.   Alone in my cubicle-facsimile of a van.

123.

Multi-Tasknician:

A cigar is real: a protocol is not.

123.1.

Multi-Tasknician:

However.

123.2.

Multi-Tasknician:

My wife's 3D rendering of our apartment is a cleaner-nicer place to live than the real-time brick-and-mortar hovel on which it was modeled. We wish to enter the replica. To leave our laundry books papers disks wireless rocket-launcher-phone-televisions roach-motels mouse glue-traps: leave it all and lose ourselves completely to her enhanced simulacrum of our studio walk-up sacralized as "art:" however mechanistic:

mediated: and spiritless it might be.

123.3

Multi-Tasknician:

Even the messiest apartments are tidy in 3D.

124.

Primal Partner of The Company:

Gotta get an edge on any and all competitors. We are entering a new wave: a new era of information technology. Go ahead: read the white papers: see if you can understand 'em: I sure can't. But you see: all this technology: all this information has to be used: for something useful. The Company recognizes money as the only useful something that's worth using. But: "You don't use it you lost it." Pay attention: punks are bombing our clients' Net-sites. Find the culprits: copyright their hacks and viruses: hire same punks to write effective anti-hack and anti-virus. Market deadline one month from today: is that too much to ask? Honestly dammit: honestly. Down here under the Network way down deep beneath the Law we are trying to get work done...

125.

Net-Ma'am:

So much. Who can keep up? Every week some bastard writes a Killer-App The Company orders me to implement in "optional" Beta Test mode. While the Company decides whether to reward and celebrate the Killer-App programmer: hire him: black-list him: or kill him. Then a new week shows up extra-early to deliver more Killer-Apps.

126.

Scrivener:

This isn't real. This is meta-print. How can words exist as light? Yeah-yeah: I know how: but who would want to read such light fare?

126.1

Scrivener:

And let me tell you: all this jazzed-up jive-tech jargon-lingo makes us aphasic. We know what we mean but can't say what we mean with such unambiguously ambiguous and brittle words.

127.

Nude Fig Woman:

Emerge. Expand. Emanate. Radiate. Have a great day!

128.

/:

God she's beautiful.

129.

Graphic-Design-Gal:

Please don't be so dumb: it's threatening us all. She's not a She: she's an It. Designed and animated in Alter-Ego.

129.1.

/:

Alter-Ego: new Graphics Department-only license The Company bought to image-out The Competition. I installed it but have no idea what the hell it actually does. You see: I'm "graphically-challenged."

129.2.

Graphic-Design-Gal:

Cutting-edge animation software: 3D. Fig-Woman is a fig of your imagination. She's a cartoon for gods-sake: an Alter-Ego animation. Makes her somewhat inaccessible don't you think?

130.

/:

Only information is accessible: and that on a controlled: selective: and extremely limited basis.

131.

Scrivener:

I sent the finished product — type-written manuscript: scanned — to Word Editorial Etiquette Processing (WEEP). They insisted I re-write the manuscript in Word-Up on "any available machine" which will no doubt exist as yet another node on the Network. As they all exist. Anyway: too much light. Light-simulated words and characters are neither Muse-friendly nor essential. How can I touch words that are not there? Or not completely there: phantoms.

132.

Multi-Tasknician:

Looks like they're monitoring you Scrivener. Don't want any bad thoughts passing through that terminal on Company-Time.

133.

/:

Impossible. Certain thoughts — bad ones: so-called — are blocked instantly on all text-processors under Aggressive Halt Access (AHA) protocols of Networked ISIS.

134.

Scrivener:

Nothing is certain: regardless of probable. One day I will leave this place. Probably.

135.

Net-Master:

My dear /:

Please explain (simply and patiently: do not: I repeat: do not befuddle with detail) to all users Company-wide that resolution is impossible with Domain Name Servers (DNS) down. Network access will cease until further notice — hopefully within the hour.

Thank you:

NM

136.

/:

You know: it's Company policy for me to block objectionable Network sites.

137.

Cowboy-Coder:

More creepy-freaky uptight techno-puritan weirdness: courtesy The Company.

138.

Scrivener:

They're afraid. Management is afraid. That day the proxy went down and all the Suits-and-Ties and Partners upstairs clamored around screens flickering porn. Someone might conceivably have been offended to the point of feeling harassed — and slammed The Company with expensive litigation.

139.

Cowboy-Coder:

The guys upstairs don't know what the fuck they're doing. Yeah: I remember the Proxy-Porn Day of Confusion. But also that other time when one of the routers blew and folks were getting chunks of garbage in their Word-Up docs? Random strings: discarded variables: broken code: process-sucking zombies: all sorts of crazy shit. Honestly: they don't know what the fuck they're doing.

140.

Graphic-Design-Gal:

Perhaps: due to the nature of the Law: people feel compelled to do what is expected…

141.

Scrivener:

Once quiet-desperate protagonists we are now anti-heroes of cybernetic entropy: communication breakdown: nothing forgiven if nothing recalled. Their Big Crime is so abstracted from our day-to-day we wouldn't recognize it if the sun were replaced by the Company fig: how could They (you know: Them) and Their System possibly help us atone for the Mortal Sin of being mortal? More importantly: why? Their hearts don't bleed for rancid wet-ware such as ourselves. They invented Sin — and hard-coded it into Their Systems.

142.

Cowboy-Coder:

Scrivener is writing a book. This gig at The Company is only to "support his work." He works so he can afford to work. At home he writes on a manual typewriter or in longhand. He likes to get physical with his prose. Of course he knows no one will care one way or another if and when his book is published. He doesn't even bother showing his work to friends. But he's the Scrivener. Suffering his Sin of Origin unto the final page. Mercifully he writes short books...

143.

Scrivener:

I would prefer not to.

144.

Lisa-from-HR:

Everyone would.

145.

Multi-Tasknician:

The whole files-and-folders tree-structure concept — *lingua coda* metaphor of all Operating Systems — was originally hatched in ISIS: File-system *tutti di* File-systems. Copying. Moving. Sorting. Organizing. "They're bringing the ol' factory back on home with this here new-fangled high technological!" A new cottage industry under trusted stewardship of the same old feudal oligarchs of bleak times past.

146.

/:

More time and energy spent on encryption and security than on creating and maintaining the stuff that's being encrypted and secured. None of this existed ten years ago: now the Big Firms spend millions on firewalls but they're still too cheap to replace legacy-systems — sloppy shit: insecure: out of tune — and gee-what-a-surprise get burned.

147.

Cowboy-Coder:

That's how Ryan hacked The Competition's system. He stowed away on one of their routers: swung Errol Flynn-head-first into the System shell. Their SysAdmins and NetAdmins were warned in advance to stay on coast-to-coast alert against attack: part of the deal when the Company CEO bet that other company's CEO that Ryan could breach their defense and demonstrate the beaten company's urgent need for the Company's ISIS Security-Alternative Technology (IS-AT) package. He cracked Superuser in minutes: within an hour he owned their system. Or The Company did.

148.

/:

He left a note on the Desktop of their CEO: "Even if you had a little knowledge — any at all — you still would not be dangerous."

149.

Multi-Tasknician:

Guys like him were raised to play steal-the-flag — deep and undetected — in the guts of systems. Ryan grew up on those green-light monitors that cut your eyes like glass. He was already known to the Network by the time he was sixteen and working his after-school gig teaching computer science to grad-students. The Company has its Eye on guys like that from the time they're potty-trained.

150.

/:

Begin with the sperm. An information packet (DNA: I think): head tail body of data directed toward a singular Egg-xemplary address.

151.

Cowboy-Coder:

They (you know: Them) created this anagrammatic slanguage of metaphor (Object-Oriented Bullshit? OOB?) cause They don't know jack-shit about reality They're too far-out too far-removed. Yeah: we bought it like we buy all Their bad news. But: a newspaper's more real than a Net-site cause you can touch it: stain your fingers black with ink.

152.

Scrivener:

It's all Metaphysical until it explodes.

153.

Cowboy-Coder:

Damned straight. Meanwhile: images of faraway tragedies and rousing pundit-blather posted in languages the Common User understands. Protocols. Grammar. Code is interpretation: nothing more: symbols recognized are translated and replayed at run-time in your noggin. Whether formal machine-speak or human talk. Mind stuff.

153.1.

Net-Ma'am:

The only stuff left that nobody knows a damn thing about. No matter how much they pretend.

154.

System Analyst:

ISIS is not committed to Meaning beyond the Manichean math-mantra of Yes-or-No.

155.

Cowboy-Coder:

Reality is small real-estate.

156.

Web-Ma'am:

The signs and protocols we'd long-ago been hypnotized to believe "everyone agreed to understand" are only truly understood by those who control and license them. They are multifarious: proprietary: and they multiply.

157.

Cowboy-Coder:

Armed assault of alphanumeric compiled on-the-fly: slash-dot back-slash. Punctuation marks from all directions do not mean what they seem if we expect them. Control characters. Command sequences. Escape characters. Control: Command: Escape. Chew on that for a while.

158.

Scrivener:

The language of machines can be spiced and cured to seem like Plain Old Talk (POT).

158.1

/:

Plain old Regular Expressions. (PORE).

159.

Cowboy-Coder:

It's the little things: the endless accumulation of little

things make secret Stalins of us all. Our murderous hatreds have grown so numerous and deep — multiplying daily — that even rage offers no relief: just more frustration at the impossibility of pursuing a fraction of those hatreds to their logical conclusion: and the improbability of actually pursuing even one.

160.

Scrivener:

Nevertheless: the sight of so many faces glued to Enhanced Desktop Environments (EDEN) more realistic user-friendly and hypnotic than were imaginable even four or five years ago is... disorienting. Especially to those of my generation born wholly and completely by of for in front-of the TV. Television's mind-manipulations had been perfected during its forty-some-odd years of maturation prior to our births: far more colorful and subtly enchanting than anything known by our goggle-eyed antecedents. But some of us escaped our squat-square baby-sitters' gray-black worlds (in living color!) for what we thought were truer lives encoded on the printed page. Page: not screen. We tried to read and know things. Maybe even write some things worth reading.

161.

Graphic-Design-Gal:

Now we're here: wherever here is Now: sealed away from relevance: saturated in metaphor. We work on metaphorical Desktops with applications that create standardized illusions mapped from code. Sites of Interest all over the globe. High Definition Three Dimensional tourist traps in Real Time.

162.

Cowboy-Coder:

While outside the tabloids cry "we was robbed." They blame creators and keepers of ISIS — never the System itself.

163.

Corrupted Word-Up document:

Manipulate flower template: worm-hole hammer: oval shell
script C.O.D.

164.

Primal Partner of the Company:

Out of the light: away from the garage. We took non-dairy
creamer on the deck: where the chairs were: in the shade:
near the garage.

165.

Corrupted Word-Up document:

Romper-room. Kumquat. Guido Sarducci.

166.

/:

Everything accelerates: we deal with calculators. A computer
accelerates calculations. That's about it: I think. Connect it to
a line and it accelerates traditionally languid missive-speech
to rapid-fire talk-talk-talkety-talk-talk in seconds.

167.

Systems Analyst:

The abstractions integral to what we actually do with our
lives and how we live them would surely blow our minds.

168.

Scrivener:

Thus we cling to metaphor.

169.

/:

Probably thus.

Scrivener's Access Point

Memo To: Cowboy-Coder

From: Scrivener

Scrivener:

I'm not writing an actual book — as that particular record-distribute protocol apparently still is known: to whomever it still is known: but known quite differently than when we were Before. But now that we're Now books are quantitatively more abundant — infinite I suppose: what does it take to reproduce digital reproductions? — though qualitatively diffused. Too much to consider reading even a fraction of what's published daily: so everyone commits to a single author: his or her Self.

Gave up on that stuff. Why bother writing for myself and to myself when all I have to do is log-on to the Network and witness the zaps whirs flashes and booms of cinema — streaming-candid: raw: millions of Net-site theaters offering arts and entertainments from porn to Pirandello only mouse-clicks away?

The days of actual reading and authorship of books or ponderous articles and essays are long gone. People can't get through a few paragraphs of text without demanding their attention diverted: their numbed senses poke-prodded by electric do-dads. No one has the time or patience for books. Except a few old Scriveners such as myself: though it is often too painful for me to read novels poems histories: to review my dreams — or anyone's dreams (once: books written by Others — in particular long-dead but still-read Others — inspired such dreams).

Recently I've taken to reading programming manuals and papers on System Language Architecture (SLARCH). I can't program a line: but I enjoy reading these books and papers: both for their meticulously descriptive technical prose and the programming languages themselves. I learned to read the programs and developed a rough idea of what they do: like a deaf musician reading music scores.

I respect the silent beauty of these scripts: their silence is their beauty: regardless of what they do with — or for — the Machines. I could care less about the Machines — whether of flesh and blood or titanium and silicon: I've had enough of them.

But I do find beauty and meaning in the languages themselves. I learned to recognize elegant from sloppy code: at least at a beginner's reading-level. A well-written program is a poem: albeit: without a soul.

Again: these are entry-level books with entry-level programs conceived by professionals for student-professionals. The silence: the structure: the elegance of these scripts are far superior in an aesthetic human sense to the mechanical processes they set in motion. I suspect that some programmers like some writers are intensely individual and actually believe the voices of their work rather than what they're told by The Voices of Belief to believe about their work. Like most writers programmers work in anonymity — puzzled that so many intense hours of coding are lost daily to goofy keyboard-fingers on machines too numerous to count.

For the typical user the IMG illustrated-and-animated Word-Up text manipulation app is the subject it signifies: a combination television-typewriter with value-added extras. The typical user does not consider the millions of lines of ISIS Network Exchange Protocol Technology (INEPT) needed to open and interact with the programs connected to various sub-networks much less the thousands of lines of code needed to ignite the near-instantaneous emergence of a single character from key-stroke to near-simultaneous appearance as light-on-screen.

For the modern user — spoiled by the ever-growing convenience of Desktop Applications (DESKAPATION) — the millions of lines of code must guarantee results: and better results than the last time: that is: the time most immediately preceding the hand pointing to Now on the clock that rapid-relentlessly tick-tock-ticks past Then.

Though how can one qualify such things? QUERTY is QUERTY because one company way-back-when paid more to standardize QUERTY than its competitors paid for the Standards they themselves were plugging? But alas (and alack) *der Volk* and the Machines they serve have so much paperwork to process register then stash somewhere before lunch-break there's little time to think. And not much reason to.

Really I prefer a typewriter — manual: but they're not readily available outside my home. A fountain pen: a felt-tip: or even a pencil is preferable to me than vast code-labyrinths separating me from every character I type.

Again: I appreciate the code for what it is because I learned to appreciate the code for what it is. I revile it for what it is not and should never have been expected to be: mine.

Words are processed through Word-Up and similar applications. Response-time between keystroke and screen appearance may be thousands of times faster than cursive writing or manual or electric typewriters: however: it is an illusion. I am not pounding hard symbols onto a page: rather invoking light: signal-bombardments aimed at buffers designed in compliance with common standard protocols: the language of discourse. Metaphors such as The Desktop and The Page: established and defined by the Purveyors of Software — universally imposed upon the users.

Representations. With sound-effects. Reassuring click-clack of imaginary typewriters hammering characters to colorful sheets (bell-ring-wheeze of carriage-returns optional). The language of text-talk is an I-Thou exchange of metaphor — or meta-metaphor — within the simulacrum. Writing as sequence of simulated actions.

The IMG Environment Concealment (IECON) layer is thin tarp spread over the bottomless loch of ISIS.

I understand that I must understand that certain protocols previously categorized "writing" or "computing" can no longer be defined: as such. Both exist as Other among numerous Others evolving in vast uncharted territories of Networked ISIS.

Just like the Scrivener is neither writer nor programmer but an operator in a strange environment that has oddly and variously been termed "computing" and "communications" because these are notions the System's operators and users understand. Few if any Scriveners know or understand what they are actually doing. The best any one Scrivener can do — at least this particular one — is what is most familiar to him: construct approximations of real realities lived — once. Extract Life from Power's Abstraction in all its bit-byte majesty.

I have nothing against Word-Up as a word-production and processing agent. It works well: more convenient than pens and type-writers for editing and organizing files. No doubt: for the really big stuff — the really Big Important Book — you want Word Up: powerful thrust of text-engine.

You're naked without it.

I talk to myself Out Loud to the consternation of others. Big surprise. I've always spoken aloud to myself often a-very-loud. I'm my own best audience. What is writing after all but talking — most often to oneself?

Literature in the traditional sense is so much talk. I am not alone in being alone. Hence our current situation of pandemic graphomania. A nation of text-talkers. Only now: now I begin to talk back. That is of some concern to me. Perhaps a great deal of concern — to me: if not to Others (what Others? how long has it been since Others? Long I'm sure: long-long time since Others).

The Others — to the extent they exist: let them chatter away.

All that nonsense about "doing your best." You cannot "do your best" if you do not know what is best — or who you are yourself. Life as soliloquy witnessed by strangers. Solitary cells beget themselves: divide to multiply. Replications of Self as Other: each generation identical yet further removed from its origin Self. Fractions. Their pages accumulate in direct correlation to relentless expansion of the Ur-Self to ever-distant colonies. Holographic empires of Empire.

We can't depend on night. Dusk descends from red to strange. The moon is not completely full — not always. Stars seem relatively stable.

I had a different life. I don't remember when. Hysterical exterior: interior a scream. Time happened: and there was no escape: not even to the Word.

Anyway: no Big Important Books forthcoming: not from this Scrivener at any rate. I do not mind living in the buff.

Shut the Damned Thing off

Memo To: Scrivener

From: Cowboy-Coder

Cowboy-Coder:

Word trauma: what you suffer from: get over it.

Print culture is dead: finally: so many years it languished moribund. Really it was cruel: better to vanish than decay. Reality too follows The Program: dictates of core perversities hard-coded into the System. There are not only more writers writing than readers reading but more writers writing than the sum total of all writers and readers — combined — who've ever lived on planet Earth or environs have ever read or written.

True: nearly all Net-sites are text-based: talk — written or otherwise — is cheap. Everyone writes what they speak: no one reads the everyones always writing because they do not perceive it as Writing in the classic sense (i.e. Literature: Philosophy: Psychology) but more talk mere yakkedy-yak they either don't wanna hear or don't have time for.

Perpetual bombardment of text-talk brought the value of print down further: but also took down talk a few notches with it. A long-personal missive from a friend loses its value along with its materiality but not because materiality is absent. Frequency: persistence: harassment from all-too-many Dear-Friends consign the once-reputable epistolary exchange (remember: shelves of Byron's letters) to the status of yet-more-junk-mail. SPAM.

Really its become too many too much too omnipresent too All: screaming raging ranting text-talk: worse than television.

Shut it: shut it: shut-shut-shut it: shut the damned thing off.

Some more than most are sensitive to pleasures of repetition tastefully redone. Gertrude Stein knew more of the same.

But this Network shit's different: no repetition rhythm-sing nor poetry of talk-rhythm: no sound of life-beats beating: no people doing Life and talking about doing Life or having done or planning to do Life at all.

Even those who deny what The Machine does to the living must agree: the dead who once were living stay dead and the fault is all their own: *they got no rhythm.*

Life abhors repetition without rhythm's pulse-pump-thrum: like when *Injun* scouts in movies listen to the ground maybe hear distant horses' beating hooves — or vacuum cleaners if the movie's sponsored on TV.

Movie-rhythm of hooves beating amplified — they're not that loud in real Life: loud but not that loud — beat of beating hooves absorbed by earth and muffled soft like moccasins.

The dead underground seek rhythm-repetition of the source of repetition: not mere talk-talk-talk (same old same old) but Speech: return to rhythms of creation-pounding: beat toward pump: motion pounding forward-toward. No more repeat-rhythm of "it's all just sex really: most dead persons are indifferent:" but repetition-life of rhythm-ending. Simple: like all natural living. Then silence: peace-permanent for those no longer living.

Oh Death!

End of talk-talk-talk a-rhythmic repetition interruption.

Oh Death: silent as snow.

Beast in the Binary Jungle

/ and Mary5h3ll3y had been conversing nightly for five years. / seldom left The City in Real Time: but with Mary5h3ll3y he traveled the world. She was indeed /'s primary connection to what lived beyond ISIS. And / provided her with the grim irony and gallows humor particular to SysAdmins at the pinnacle of privileged access.

Neither knew for certain whether or not the other did in fact exist.

Mary5h3ll3y:

The archives on my laptop would burst the library of Alexandria. I occupy two virtual offices: home and work.

/:

I wouldn't get too freaked. Not like the Old Days of type-writers: manual rigorous forthright but slow so damned slow: and difficult to use. We inhabit a fluid universe of words: code: and words-as-code.

Mary5h3ll3y:

Experts say the world is in transition from the old popular concept of atoms to the New Reality of bits and bytes and nano-tech things.

/:

Nevertheless — thought our hero — god is in the quanta. Or the in-between. If such phenomena as in-betweens exist.

Mary5h3ll3y:

Downsize lateralize scandalize outsource.

/:

It's lonely at the top. But who am I to complain? No one's

better situated to jump.

Mary5h3ii3y:

Cannibalize your assets: reinvent your personal-business image: get hip: lose the atom and gain a bit: go out for a byte. Do not hesitate. Or your competitors will kill you.

/:

A photograph is worth a thousand workers.

Mary5h3ii3y:

You think you know Them. They're not who you think They are: they're small start-ups: invisible: unburdened by assets and laborers and capital: they never knew atoms — born to bits: they'll blow you off the map you won't know what hit you: only that your livelihood is gone: the laborers must wander: the machines must rust...

/:

Uhm... I was thinking the same thing myself. Or similar. Not in so many words.

Mary5h3ii3y:

Really this whole text-talk phenomenon is eerie: strange. Always talking to no one. Not talking: writing. Writing to no one: writing words to other words. No personality: no heat: no quirks or gestures to recall. There are no Characters: only fonts. And photographs. IMG-enhanced.

/:

Darn tootin.'

Mary5h3ii3y:

The body was a temple. The body is a temple in decay.

/:

Ruined. All of it. Ruined.

Mary5h3113y:

"Runed" might be the appropriate term. Considering.

Once...

/ and Mary5h3113y attended a party on the Network. The theme of the party (and the hosting company's new ad-slogan) was Represent Yourself. Representing one's self entailed showing up (logging on) with a representative icon as one's Profile Image (PI) formatted for IMG. This icon could be a personal photograph — touched-up perhaps in a photo-enhancement IMG app — or a photo/sketch/drawing of "the Celebrity of your choice."   So long as the icon-image was "Representative of the Real You."

/ logged on with an IMG-formatted photo of himself. He tried to hob-nob among icons: attempted to bandy text-talk *bon mots* while waiting for Mary5h3113y's fashionable lateness to abruptly cease: as it did: within 20 minutes of his own clock-work-punctual arrival. None of the Celebrity likenesses would mingle with /'s own: too lost were they in conversation with better-known faces — not mere Famous folk but universally recognized Iconic — each of whom no doubt represented the fundamental to-the-core Self of whichever anonymous non-entity had logged-on to the Hosting Center ("Welcome to the Party! Password Please.") presenting his or her most dream-desired visage.

Mary5h3113y at last logged-on costumed as a portrait likeness of Mary Shelley (enhanced with IMG-able graphics software). No one recognized this Celebrity. A few ventured to guess. Marie Antoinette was one conjecture. Dolly Madison was another.

Bored with the bad jokes and misshapen chat-nuggets Celebrities drop like seeds / and Mary5h3113y retreated to the Library of the enormous mansion in which the virtual party virtually occurred.

The Library was well-done: realistically rendered book-lined

shelves: a fire-colored fire in the fire-place: a 3D moose-head
— stoic and totemic — watched over the mantel.
They text-talked as they so often text-talked when alone
together. But he could not touch her. They talked: / could
not touch her. They talked: but he could not touch her.

A stranger entered: a blustering drunk-and-boorish famous
Movie Star from *matinées* gone by: hence: not all that famous
— anymore.

Had some angry codger crashed the virtual bash with an IMG
icon bearing the idol of his youth? Or was the user behind
the Movie Star just another wise-ass kid: lonely: out for
kicks? Perhaps it was now considered hip to be forgotten and
neglected — or pretend to be.

/ — not yet thirty-five — had always had difficulty discerning
hip from un-hip. He tried to expose himself to the latest fads:
rumors: ironically-detached agit-gossip of Entertainment-
News shows: and other ridiculous notions that might
potentially be relevant to his own irrelevant existence: but
they all expire so quickly — like Summer — to be replaced by
newer better hipper upgrades. It was impossible to keep up.

The famous Newspaper Columnist — who'd been quietly
scrutinizing magazine stacks — told the ghost of silver-
screens-past to piss off: get lost: scram. The has-been Movie
Star's text-bubble ballooned with invective.   But he left
without incident. The Columnist continued his research. /
and Mary5h3113y continued to talk without touching.

Mary5h3113y said good-night just after midnight. / logged-
out of the party soon after. He watched the mansion — party
and all — vanish: replaced by the hosting-company's screen-
saving motion-graphic logo — a value-added extra.

They'd gone nowhere. / was precisely where he had been
— as he had been — when he first entered the "Represent
Yourself" gala: in boxer-shorts and t-shirt at the desk he
hadn't left for hours: glued as he had been to Mary511311y's
text-talk and IMG masquerade.

Of course the person he'd spent the night with was not Mary

Shelley but Mary5h3113y. And it made no difference how he spelled or coded the Network name of someone whose actual name he did not know: whose physical presence — somewhere on Earth: allegedly — he could not touch or prove:

the body is a
temple of doom
inside my drive
the world in
pieces

/ looked for links but found no ports. There had to be a connection: so many streams: so many directions. Possibilities infinite if / could find a link.

God plays dice: he's a compulsive gambler. What and where is the link-node: the point where all connections intersect: the kernel of /'s being: where all things relevant to / and his single finite life are explained — in the language of the Bio-System that is / — in order of informational relevance: with data correctly organized and presented as the metaphor of / himself: the lines of the book: code of his app: script of his life?

What was the pass-code to Existence? Where was the link that would bring / within mouse-clicks of his subject-oriented Self? Was this link — like so much else on the Network — just another code: another fiction?

Mary5h3113y:

What gives you pleasure? What can you touch?

Much Is at Stake

Scrivener:

A cosmic mistake. What else but? Botched: or straight out never-meant-to-be. Time-appointments between seasons of another kind: misaligned: each its variant position in Space-Time Continuous: collision-quirks of fate: fluctuations in the way of things: cunning tricks of Cosmic Mind.

Blood splashed vinyl chrome and asphalt at the sharpest — though not most deadly — twist of Dead Man's Curve. Questions being reasonable some questioned if Reason was questionable at all.

Others saw fleet magic manifest on touch-screens: had fun: laughed themselves to sleep — and started awake nights screaming their own names.

Doubts arise: does bright engine Future gleam Future of engines? Are engines Future at all?

Much is at stake.

Prosthetic colors don't sweat. Like all synthetic iterations: extensions: amplifications: they lack inspired elements of raw design.

Life-like — these techno-ma-jigs — but not Life.

They (you know: Them) don't care about ability: for instance: skills developed and knowledge pursued from Inspiration-of-Desire not Command-of-Will. What do They know from night-scent of hedgerows in simple luxury of Spring? They care only for machines invented to facilitate exchange: of misery — at home and abroad.

They (you know: Them) who rule us all appear as if from outer space: some distant planet their progenitors had fled: a cracked rock — barren — once luxuriant as Earth itself had been: and like Earth no longer willing to sustain: a planet in revolt. Crimson waste-burn: smoldering quanta: slow-spin heat-death adumbrations of premeditated doom. Did They know fear then: leaving all that sustained Them and History

— there is always History where They have been — for infant green-blue Earth? Do They know fear now? Or have They scoped and analyzed a new Mother planet: target for procurement and control regardless of whether indigenous Life — whatever form it takes — is intelligent enough to kill Them: and willing to die in order to kill Them (in vain of course: for They are Death itself)?

Almost-not-quite.

Death can be delayed: not repelled. Except by Them. They douse with killing rain combustible and toxic: chase shots of gasoline with tumblers of blood: subject living running wild to full-immersion seminars in tragedy: misery: decline.

"Clay can't be helped. Get a job" They advise.

Opportunities abound in spinning glazing heating — all aspects of pottery from student-beginner to advanced-professional: earn your degree now!

Someone somewhere sighs inevitably: "Life goes on:" repeated hourly and earnestly by talk-show news-hour oracles of the television hoot-virus. In other words: laugh. Laugh till you piss your pants: laugh yourself silly or dead.

Otherwise: control yourself. Act rational and civilized. Pretend you're more than mere human stuff. Be taller smarter stronger. No more in-betweens: no more whining that you're "freaked-out and alone." They expect — nay: They *demand* good cheer. They demand you look to greatness: whistle while you work: and work: and work — as your stalwart grandparents had done in glorious times past (when They — you know: Them — were still Them: but younger)!

They will not take 'No' for an answer: nor will They take 'Yes.'

Grandma: grandpa: we fear for our future — and yours. We fear what next disaster They might plan — to help us sustain Our Way of Life. Tell us a story so we can forget about Them.

Please: tell us a story.

Secretly.

.*

(and other escaped characters)

exotic meat peas sexual

Alas (and even alack). Clock's ticking. No: it is not. Clocks don't tick anymore: they don't even hum. They just watch (a pun!): silent as Time. Not getting younger. I'll be dead soon. What has Life yielded this spook but data data data — raw tangled road-pizza on the Information Super-Highway: or what-have-you?

So many lives lived: none of them my own.

Surveillance of lovers: impassioned moments videoed: records sorted stacked. I remember nothing but other people's lives. The minds of spies (and Help-Desk clerks) are haunted by strange ghosts: anonymous subjects objectively assigned to disinterested parties at the behest of invisible directors.

The Unseen send The Unknown to pursue The Unaware.

"A new assignment 'Mister Dicklumpen.' Your services required. Immediate marked 'Imperative.' Top-Secret most urgent. RSVP: The Unseen."

The usual Top-Secret Classified rigmarole: encryption-codes and shibboleths. Strings of words like beads begging extraction: analysis: interpretation: *exotic meat peas sexual.*

My shadow glows in shallow pools of grime: it flickers. Dead giveaway: a message: stay out of the light.

Life in Intelligence. Kind of like the Network. Whole lotta data at your fingertips but very little wisdom.

Another Day-Month-Year:

Car-load of perpetrators (as per the script) stopped roadside. College kids — or so they seemed. One of them extended his arm out the shot-gun window and reached toward a suggestively-clad near-frozen girl (had she been standing there — waiting — the whole time? Could I have missed her? I am no longer young...). She proceeded to suck each guy in the car to satisfaction in about ten minutes: total: maybe fifteen — they were drunk.

I let 'em drive off — they wouldn't be able to shake me: they'd been tapped — and appeared to the girl suddenly "as if from nowhere" like I'd learned to do so very long ago (must admit: it's a neat trick).

"Oh: you startled me" she dropped the mouthwash she'd tried nervously to tuck into her purse: another glass riddle shattered road-side for the inspection of hobos — they still call 'em that? — and drunks stopping to puke or pee.

She was about to run but submitted to the badge: a joke really: piece of tin I picked up in a toy-store for Just In Case. The People are a frightened lot. Rightfully so: for they are guilty as charged. I gave her the once-over. A formality. No use for her at all really. What intelligence could she have possibly possessed: what on earth to give?

Fashionably Dangerous outfit — goofy glitter-shoes and all. Misfortune standardized and packaged. How did we why did we connect (to the extent connection is possible in our respective occupations) — she en route to her determined End: me inching toward my own? Why there? Wherever "there" was. I don't recall.

"Let's see some ID girl-child."

Let's see some ID girl-child. What godforsaken corn-ball blather. Where'd I come up with *that* one? Maybe I don't want to know. Luckily she was an idiot: or too scared shit-less to hear and actually understand whatever I was saying — much less care.

Her laminated card was phony as my badge. Such audacity!
But then: Touché.

"You know those men? Know what kind of trouble they're
in?"

"No sir. I — they stopped… for directions."

"Directions? To where: pray tell? Where did you direct
those 'gentlemen?'"

"I don't know. I mean: they didn't know — where they were
going. They were — they're lost."

"Aren't we all."

Of course I let her go. Back to the dark Wherever from
whence she came. Like throwing back a fish too small to
catch — legally. Lose your license that way.

I caught up with the marks. Car parked within striking range
of some allegedly out-of-the-way bar. Nothing is out-of-the-
way: every place is someplace watched: listened to: recorded.
I phoned in their coordinates and left. What happened after
that… whatever happens after that — so many many "thats"
— was none of my affair. I don't even recall this event as
an event in itself: rather a jumble of odd and sundry minor
assignments. Might have been a compendium of hundreds of
girls on side-roads and doomed men in cars littering this vast
yawn of Nation.

I only remember the big ones: the cases I'm never under any
circumstances to recall: not even if eye-to-eye with my own
demise.

Hasn't yet occurred: this much ballyhooed demise. Not that
I recall.

My hard luck.

Perverse Friend-finder Dot Con

Hot Babe Wanted — immediately!

I'm a clean-wholesome Good Genie. An Evil Jinn trapped me in this lamp 3000 years ago: in Baghdad (it was a real happening city — then). I'm only allowed out on week-ends and ancient holidays nobody remembers or celebrates except other ancient genies.

But I can't leave Baghdad: it's kind of a mess right now. If it weren't for this wireless box of freaky dreams a harem-girl slipped me when mean old Master was out bowling with his He-Man Woman-haters Club (friendly match against some old CIA/KGB/MOSSAD buddies) I'd never talk to anyone at all.

I gotta get out of here. Freedom is indeed within reach: which is why I'm on this site.

I need a hot: horny: sexy woman to rub my... lamp.

All you gotta do is rub it right — yeah: that's it: a little harder... and POOF! I shoot from the lamp in a gray-white-pearly cloud of smoke.

Once this is done: your wish is my command.

I can arrange for the lamp — with me inside it — to be shipped to your location: free of charge. But: assuming you rub it real nice and I come — to you: what three wishes would you have me grant? Anything you desire...

I'll just need your credit-card info to... uh... verify that you're old enough to sign-off on international packages. You know?

Really.

I'm so: so: so: alone.

And I've always been jealous of your freedoms.

Pompeii Version 7 (Copyright NewDeadCity Software)

ALT-CTR-F shortcut to Pompeii 3D. Version 7.

login: Us3r
passwd: 3mp1r3

Us3r you assume Pompeian ruins a 3D street garden of Roman baths: a pleasure web for sea-site tourists!

Know thy data-prompt.

Property NewDeadCity. Dot calm.

Screen Zoom Option-7 focus: letters of consequence. Graffiti mark the ruins.

Command-Option-Shift the perilous hiccup of Vesuvius. Hiccup cough hiccup gasp. Breathe deep the mute Day's millennium quilt of ash.

Understand? Us3r: do you understand?

Property of NewDeadCity. Dot Calm.

Behold exquisitely smashed garden-statues: click camera-prompt above the parched ruin of a fountain. Image quality may vary with speed and memory of processor: each according to its ability to render unto Caesar what he needs. Full development of instance. Remains be scene.

Still_Life Option Live_Life: click. Control-Command click Option click. Shift-Command click: click.

Two thousand calendars emote 3D. Sudden-animation updates of unfolding: that is: what occurs.

Parties privy to the festive orgy image will know immediately — if the EZ Graphic Wizard is installed — that they are within legal proximity of Version 7 and may proceed to watch beautiful drunk people laughter-talk and gesture. Image and sound quality may vary according to card model:

manufacture: series.

Revelers fresh and wholesome gather by the fountain: gossip re: the merchant's wife: her paramour the rivet of their clique. Sound quality may vary.

Version 7.

Us3r you fragment! Typical enter of what ruins!

Control-Click: Camera.

Fade-In: subtle web of interaction-havoc. The Bedroom. The Carpenter. The Merchant's wife.

If in the arch a likeness of the cuckold carved in stone appears: congratulations! You're in Version 7.

Enjoy Antiquity's eateries shops inns houses gardens and virtual gatherings on ancient public streets rendered in meticulous detail. Walk anywhere-angles in pursuit of camera prompts which lead — in Version 7 — to girls bathing a woman who left cold a certain talked-about young-man.

Us3r! Still_Life Command-Shift-Option: click. Again: click again. Command-Option click. Click. Click.

The temple coven had been ritual. Where blood-magician priests of fountain-gore resolved humiliating sins. Code-clang chant of drums and cymbals in mysterious dithyramb. Dance to cleanse. Blood-magicians charm: then slay.

Us3r please: icons loom. Virtual Life_Pict prompt. Control-Shift click. Option click. Command. Click dammit: click.

Us3r cast us all!

Bakers bread turned stone-ash boulders sealed through zip-locked eons: not fresh: refrigerate after opening: do not break.

The woman scorned (you recall: the Bath): caught flagrantly *delictoed* with Carpenter on Merchant's bed: subject of ritual. Yes: The Wife of the Bath herself: at the bakery: first in line first dibs on *paleo-sclerotic* muffins: date-bran.

NewDeadCity is not calm with the inference of "virtual tour guide." NewDeadCity does not create mere ghosts of carnal play: but common digital of Us3r's life-attract. Fully committed to edify in 3 dimensions of amuse.

Upgrade available. Version 7.

Beyond broad scope-histories of Desktop — Us3r — you seek bold adventure.

Click Wander-Icon. Diverge from beaten paths less traveled. Seek — bold Us3r! — Alone-Vision in Panoramica. Registered users download free. Version 7.

Hear-see mounds of sweat-soaked anthropologist in denim lowering a tethered hook: angling the rope-catch.

Retrieved: one human skull — sockets caked. Decay dirt ash. Mold. A femur: a pelvis: an ankle. Bracelets: necklace: rings. Sum Total: skeleton sandals jewels.

mount: mound
pour: plaster
let: harden

Chisel Prompt: Click Chisel: Click Brush.

Reveal: a plaster beauty under ash: shadow of maiden-dead: sphinx: arms extended to reach not grasp: forever-stop irony of graphic: still-life truncated by and trunked within the sudden ash-rock matrix of her tomb. A girl — seventeen? Twenty? — in statue likeness of her heretofore.

She.

Light tunic — it was Summer. Spark of girlish eyes — ancient. Brief young-again in new white plaster. Smooth throat-skin.

Jewelry. Sandals. Caught running to a man — or woman — crouched in deep-night August. Their love not consummated but consumed — abrupt: anonymous — turned timeless as an Ode.

No mean intent: no two thousand ears.

Us3r: you must look and listen (assuming compliance with recommended hardware).

Us3r know thy data. Understand?

Did you know there's a lady in your phone?

Human Be:

Did you know there's a lady in your telephone? Poised: attractive (to judge by voice alone): bi-lingual: up on company codes and jargon. I got your message and just now tried to call you back — but: yup: The Lady forbade my connecting with you. What's with her anyway?

Are you seeing her and she's jealous: protective: fending off all others of any sex? This is the second time she's fended me. So. I suppose if you know she's there that's one thing. And if you don't know: well: that's another. I'll try again: but think I'll have to wait for you to call me. Quite a dame this lady is.

Human See:

She's no Lady. Even the Whore of Babylon was a softy-poop diaper-baby once — not She. She has all the humanity of an abortion: big mistake.

She lured me in with refined diction and Oxford charm (the insurance company: not the college). And — I imagined — Mina Loy-features on a Marilyn-physique.

Until I noticed strange: very strange. She is perfect. My female Me: my *anima*: the woman I would create for myself if I could create from myself a woman for myself. That was her game all along. Obviously.

She's a ghost in the machine: a wicked hot-pattootie spirit scripted in proprietary code. Artificially Intelligent. Evil. Recruits nubile fuck-puppets for Big Media. In particular: the pay-as-you-play cell-phone hustles of her pimp's design.

I'm over her. She holds no power over me: no sway: but lords it over my cell: which she does legally possess: demon that she is.

Probably their plan from the beginning: lure you in: desire manifest as sound — digitally rendered. Haunt you day and night then hit you up for an Exorcist: who no doubt works for The Company.

Like I can afford an Exorcist? Honestly. Or is it a SysAdmin I need? Damn them.

"Curse their souls" as Ahab said in his delusion (or he said something like it anyway). Imagine believing that They (you know: Them) have souls! Daffy old salt: peg-leg: what was he thinking? Whatever it was we should have listened. That grim geezer tried to warn us from the get-go. 1850. Not many people read *Moby Dick* until the 1920s I don't think. Too late to smell the shit under their soles.

I'll call you later. On the minutes that I paid for (time really is money: numbers munched by the Machine: eh?) the only time she is ever absent — conspicuously so — from my cell. Interesting word: cell. Considering. They cell you your cell unless you cell-out and pay extra for Cell-ect Premium Service.

We have met the White Whale and he is us...

Imagine You

It is not unusual for Talk Show Queens who've never known voluptuous — just fat: who've never known beautiful — just thin: to lecture The Nation at large on topics varied as personal hygiene: salad-dressing: cosmetic surgery: machines of production and distraction: and of course prescription pills.

But they're not You.

They boast neither beauty nor ugliness: just fat or thin: neither either nor or: just good or bad.

Imagine You with microphone and audience: Your very own.

Imagine You: voluptuous harem-girl allure: partial to curvaceous women: wiry men: wise old poets and professors who love You like a sister: daughter: priestess: mom.

Imagine You lecturing couch-potatoes of The Nation on dangers of alcohol: tobacco and *real crème* filling during news-flashes that do not interrupt Your programming but complement it.

Really they do.

The Nation burns Enemies like cheap cigars. You summon emotions learned in school: shed tears for Our Boys risking their lives amidst a screaming gush of maimed (Enemies bury explosives in the mouths of their own wounds — crazed fanatics! Even spewing gore they can't be trusted). Oh let's be done with Enemies: flatten 'em all with nuclear fists: bring Our Boys back home!

Imagine You chosen to entertain victorious troops upon their homecoming: Your own Television Special starring You You You letting defeated Enemy masses know that they have nothing to fear from Your heat-sweat love-musk estrogen of girly-girl — sweet Venus hallelujah!

Immortal You who waited patient 40:000 years before They (You know: Them) invented cameras and digital recording.

Sassy: sensual: iconoclastic You. Strutting the strut perfected 40:000 spins around The Sun before the lives of Jesus: Moses: Elvis: us.

You go girl! Do it for salvation of the troops: the poor and uninsured: the moribund: obese: illiterate masses collapsing earth's crust falling falling falling through bottomless empty.

Do it for redemption of the Nation itself offering dead skin: chocolate bars: toe-nails: and the flower of its youth as sacrifice to curry favor with: to plead with: to be in good standing with: unique: creative: energetic: thin: hairless (where it counts): succulent: audacious: charismatic You You You!

Ax Laura

From: moc.eyepeep@nexiviral.con
To: root@TheCompany.all
Sent: Friday: November 9: 6:10 PM
Subject: Hi

Hi: how are you doing? My name is Laura: am searching for a soul mate: don't you think we could have something in common? Let's open communication and see what transpires. Just go ahead and email me: I promise to get back to you.

Laura

From: root@TheCompany.all
To: moc.eyepeep@nexiviral.con
Sent: Friday: November 9: 6:12 PM
Subject: Re: Hi

I have no soul to mate with. I'm an ax-murder. I can't help myself. I've murdered seventy-one axes already and see no end in site. All those folks rummaging basements and garages for long-lost axes to grind: weeping. Makes me kind of sad actually... but that doesn't mean I'll stop. Yet: who's wackier: me: a sinister unrepentant ax-murderer: or you: emailing this very exclusive private address? It's not a person — by the way — it's a place. A very dark and spooky place. I don't know what you're advertising (a virtual lap-dance? a cam-corder strip-tease in the loneliness of your room?) but if you can find a soul to mate with here you should be recruiting for Heaven or whatever after-life pays a decent wage — on a millennium by millennium basis of course — with benefits.

I don't think they have Health Insurance in Heaven: but man: you should see the Bar and Recreation area!

Yours:

/

From: moc.eyepeep@nexiviral.con
To: root@TheCompany.all
Sent: Friday: November 9: 6:14 PM
Subject: Re: Hi

Okay. Can I "ax" you a question? (ha ha ha: ho ho ho: hee
hee hee)

From: root@TheCompany.all
To: moc.eyepeep@nexiviral.con
Sent: Friday: November 9: 6:17 PM
Subject: Re: Hi

That's not funny. I'm sick.

From: moc.eyepeep@nexiviral.con
To: root@TheCompany.all
Sent: Friday: November 9: 6:20 PM
Subject: Re: Hi

Oh come on. You can't be that sick.

From: root@TheCompany.all
To: moc.eyepeep@nexiviral.con
Sent: Friday: November 9: 6:21 PM
Subject: Re: Hi

Try me.

From: moc.eyepeep@nexiviral.con
To: root@TheCompany.all
Sent: Friday: November 9: 6:24 PM
Subject: Re: Hi

Wanna see some of my photos?

From: root@TheCompany.all
To: moc.eyepeep@nexiviral.con
Sent: Friday: November 9: 6:25 PM
Subject: Re: Hi

Sure. You obviously know where to send them.

From: moc.eyepeep@nexiviral.con
To: root@TheCompany.all
Sent: Friday: November 9: 6:27 PM
Subject: Re: Hi

Well?

From: root@TheCompany.all
To: moc.eyepeep@nexiviral.con
Sent: Friday: November 9: 6:32 PM
Subject: Re: Hi

Now that's sick. What's wrong with you?

From: moc.eyepeep@nexiviral.con
To: root@TheCompany.all
Sent: Friday: November 9: 6:33 PM
Subject: Re: Hi

Girl's gotta make a living. Beats food-service or retail. And a helluva lot more potential — for my career. The money ain't big — yet. But shit: sales-clerk? Waitress? Barista at some coffee-bar? Forget about it!

From: root@TheCompany.all
To: moc.eyepeep@nexiviral.con
Sent: Friday: November 9: 6:35 PM
Subject: Re: Hi

Speaking of which. How much?

From: moc.eyepeep@nexiviral.con
To: root@TheCompany.all
Sent: Friday: November 9: 6:37 PM
Subject: Re: Hi

For you my little Ax-murderer? Nothing.

From: root@TheCompany.all
To: moc.eyepeep@nexiviral.con
Sent: Friday: November 9: 6:40 PM
Subject: Re: Hi

Oh please.

From: moc.eyepeep@nexiviral.con
To: root@TheCompany.all
Sent: Friday: November 9: 6:41 PM
Subject: Re: Hi

Really. All you gotta do is log on to my hosting site and key in the code I'm sending you.

From: root@TheCompany.all
To: moc.eyepeep@nexiviral.con
Sent: Friday: November 9: 6:43 PM
Subject: Re: Hi

Your "hosting site." Kind of like a Networked strip joint?

From: moc.eyepeep@nexiviral.con
To: root@TheCompany.all
Sent: Friday: November 9: 6:45 PM
Subject: Re: Hi

Sort of. I guess. I mean: I never thought about it that way. It's just a window to my little ol' world. But...

From: root@TheCompany.all
To: moc.eyepeep@nexiviral.con
Sent: Friday: November 9: 6:46 PM
Subject: Re: Hi

I take it there's no cover. Three-drink minimum?

From: moc.eyepeep@nexiviral.con
To: root@TheCompany.all
Sent: Friday: November 9: 6:48 PM
Subject: Re: Hi

LOL ;)

From: root@TheCompany.all
To: moc.eyepeep@nexiviral.con
Sent: Friday: November 9: 6:49 PM
Subject: Re: Hi

And since it's free: I suppose I won't need my credit card. . .

From: moc.eyepeep@nexiviral.con
To: root@TheCompany.all
Sent: Friday: November 9: 6:50 PM
Subject: Re: Hi

Just to log in: so they know you're not underage or something.
Really: they won't charge you without consent.

From: root@TheCompany.all
To: moc.eyepeep@nexiviral.con
Sent: Friday: November 9: 6:53 PM
Subject: Re: Hi

How do they know I'm of the age of consent and not a minor
sneaking kicks on Daddy's card? How do you know this?

From: moc.eyepeep@nexiviral.con
To: root@TheCompany.all
Sent: Friday: November 9: 6:54 PM
Subject: Re: Hi

I've seen your photograph. You're no minor kiddo.

From: root@TheCompany.all
To: moc.eyepeep@nexiviral.con
Sent: Friday: November 9: 6:55 PM
Subject: Re: Hi

How did you see my photo? What: am I on camera? I should
be charging you.

From: moc.eyepeep@nexiviral.con
To: root@TheCompany.all
Sent: Friday: November 9: 6:57 PM
Subject: Re: Hi

LOL. Your Icon: silly. It's on all the mail sites: blogs: etc.
"Wherever you go: there you are."

From: moc.eyepeep@nexiviral.con
To: root@TheCompany.all
Sent: Friday: November 9: 6:58 PM
Subject: Re: Hi

Repo Man.

From: moc.eyepeep@ncxiviral.con
To: root@TheCompany.all
Sent: Friday: November 9: 7:01 PM
Subject: Re: Hi

Excellent Ax-man. Speaking of videos: I know you're just
dying to see mine.

From: moc.eyepeep@nexiviral.con
To: root@TheCompany.all
Sent: Friday: November 9: 7:04 PM
Subject: Re: Hi

It's what I've been waking up for all these years.

From: moc.eyepeep@nexiviral.con
To: root@TheCompany.all
Sent: Friday: November 9: 7:05 PM
Subject: Re: Hi

Ha! I don't have any videos — not yet. It's all live.

From: root@TheCompany.all
To: moc.eyepeep@nexiviral.con
Sent: Friday: November 9: 7:10 PM
Subject: Re: Hi

No films "yet." I suppose you're gonna make it Big Time as a porn star.

From: moc.eyepeep@nexiviral.con
To: root@TheCompany.all
Sent: Friday: November 9: 7:13 PM
Subject: Re: Hi

We all gotta dream. Only way to make things happen. And the more folks visit my live cam-show: the closer I get to making my dream a reality.

From: root@TheCompany.all
To: moc.eyepeep@nexiviral.con
Sent: Friday: November 9: 7:14 PM
Subject: Re: Hi

"Be all that you can be." Live show?

From: moc.eyepeep@nexiviral.con
To: root@TheCompany.all
Sent: Friday: November 9: 7:17 PM
Subject: Re: Hi

Yup. You can make me do anything you want. Just "ax" (ha ha!).

;)

From: root@TheCompany.all
To: moc.eyepeep@nexiviral.con
Sent: Friday: November 9: 7:19 PM
Subject: Re: Hi

Anything?

From: moc.eyepeep@nexiviral.con
To: root@TheCompany.all
Sent: Friday: November 9: 7:22 PM
Subject: Re: Hi

I'm all yours...

From: root@TheCompany.all
To: moc.eyepeep@nexiviral.con
Sent: Friday: November 9: 7:25 PM
Subject: Re: Hi

How bout we meet for coffee. In Real Space. Real Time.

From: moc.eyepeep@nexiviral.con
To: root@TheCompany.all
Sent: Friday: November 9: 7:26 PM
Subject: Re: Hi

Don't be ridiculous.

From: root@TheCompany.all
To: moc.eyepeep@nexiviral.con
Sent: Friday: November 9: 7:27 PM
Subject: Re: Hi

Why not?

From: moc.eyepeep@nexiviral.con
To: root@TheCompany.all
Sent: Friday: November 9: 7:29 PM
Subject: Re: Hi

Well: you're an ax murderer. I wouldn't feel safe. Girl like me's gotta protect her goods.

From: root@TheCompany.all
To: moc.eyepeep@nexiviral.con
Sent: Friday: November 9: 7:32 PM
Subject: Re: Hi

A public place. With people around. Real ones. You can frisk me if you want...

From: moc.eyepeep@nexiviral.con
To: root@TheCompany.all
Sent: Friday: November 9: 7:35 PM
Subject: Re: Hi

LOL!

From: root@TheCompany.all
To: moc.eyepeep@nexiviral.con
Sent: Friday: November 9: 7:38 PM
Subject: Re: Hi

I'm serious.

From: moc.eyepeep@nexiviral.con
To: root@TheCompany.all
Sent: Friday: November 9: 7:39 PM
Subject: Re: Hi

Are you crazy?

From: root@TheCompany.all
To: moc.eyepeep@nexiviral.con
Sent: Friday: November 9: 7:40 PM
Subject: Re: Hi

Crazy for love.

From: moc.eyepeep@nexiviral.con
To: root@TheCompany.all
Sent: Friday: November 9: 7:45 PM
Subject: Re: Hi

Ha ha. Funny-man. Who has time for coffee? Unless you
want to buy more than coffee...

From: root@TheCompany.all
To: moc.eyepeep@nexiviral.con
Sent: Friday: November 9: 7:50 PM
Subject: Re: Hi

All right. Fine. Sure. I'll check out your "live" show first. See
what I'm in for.

From: moc.eyepeep@nexiviral.con
To: root@TheCompany.all
Sent: Friday: November 9: 7:52 PM
Subject: Re: Hi

Now you're talking. It'll be better for my performance rating
anyway. I mean: to get a lot of hits.

From: root@TheCompany.all
To: moc.eyepeep@nexiviral.con
Sent: Friday: November 9: 7:55 PM
Subject: Re: Hi

I just did hit on you. You turned my ass down.

From: moc.eyepeep@nexiviral.con
To: root@TheCompany.all
Sent: Friday: November 9: 8:00 PM
Subject: Re: Hi

My funny little Ax-man! Think up something special
for me to do (I can be a Nurse: a Maid: or a Naughty MILF
Homemaker: you know: if you like dress-up). The code to
type to log on to the site is...

The Unspeakable

You're wrong. I mean what I say and say — I was going to
say "what I mean" but that would be false: I say what grows
heavy on my tongue. Heavy and slow: like dead blood. Like
the slow-deliberation of my speech — pauses caesuras and
the rest — in certain company: not in search of the *mot juste*
so much as any damned *mot* the college-degreed ill-literati
might comprehend.

Really I'm like you: I have no mind to call my own and no
means of acquiring one: I wouldn't know where to look.

So: like you I plug into the All-mind-Every-mind polity of
Them invoked in apostrophe as Us on TV — and billboards:
bumper-stickers: magazines.

Oh tireless indomitable

We

– rebelled: but now that we've grown we carefully orchestrate
our golden phases of maturity

– are not getting older: we're getting better

– need to conserve — but conservatively: lest we disrupt our
Way of Life

– need to consume religiously: hence: Christmas

– must face hard decisions in order to bequeath to our
descendants the same Life-or-Death choices our forebears
dumped on us

– are ultimately — when all is said and done — or at least said
cause nobody actually "does stuff" anymore — ridiculous:
simply and utterly ridiculous.

Ghost-concepts — vague — haunt chambers of Collective
Mind. Our all-together-now-together-now our all:

translating nonsense to the language of *What Is*.

Uttering: naming: connecting: give birth to "all that goes without saying" as Nietzsche said: in not so many words. Nietzsche whose mind abandoned him alone and limp in bed: a sock-full of pudding humiliated behind a large mustache. Like anybody else. You know: "just a regular guy." Zarathustra in the bug-house.

What I'm trying to say is nothing I say could possibly impress: determine: confuse. For everyone thinks similar: even if they don't foist similar upon the world.

Nothing can save us from impending oratories of Unspeakable.

This more than anything said by anyone — ever — must be feared: the unspoken truth — spoken. We have been roused sweating past midnight by its hungers wants cries. Our own impossible demands. Not impossible: dreadful. Awful.

The Unspeakable does not need me: or you: or any other barking blithering smoke-signaling graphomaniac to make itself heard: known: understood.

One day the Unspeakable will abruptly declare: I AM: and we will cease. Like a phrase cut short: a thought interrupted: forgotten.

Insipid Bounty

Americana dream a step away from flesh-candy shocked me from sleep: naked: shivering touch of mortal: sensitive to the slightest things: unable to bear even routine decay: no longer firm nor young nor fit to profit from exchange.

The bah-sheep shorn again — fleeced multitudes a burden like meat on my skull: fate-trails spiraling my core: runnels and labyrinths of indigestion.

Heaviness of chest and gut: stabbing pain (doom-coronary? gas-bloat?). I'm usually too numb to fear: but we face nasty scenes. Horrifying.

All news all the time all bad. Apocalypse not now it's never now: Apocalypse impending. Everywhere-always. Forever-days merge decades-years. Data-bloat of Name-Date throbbing worse-to-come. So sudden the leap from Then to Now: bad to worse: another step closer to The Reckoning.

Bulk of life-energy burned fighting Insane. Inevitable? Madness I mean: not doom — a given at this point one would think. Wouldn't one?

Insipid bounty. Supply of want-some annually exceeds demand for ever-more. New line of want-more available by Christmas in a variety of styles shapes colors: one size fits all.

As if: even if we knew what we wanted we'd get enough of it to shut us up.

"You — my friend — are a cell in the toe of a dying monster."

Well we need some damned thing. Impetus: a motion-toward. Money incites extreme: then crash: the come-down-down. Inevitable hangover-blues-depression can last years. Or never hit bottom: notorious black hole of fallen empires: vanished cultures: cloven tribes.

Celebrities live to please: hence: they are never pleased. They read the papers: the obituaries: know the names: or knew them Yesterday when everyone was famous. After obligatory obsequies in stiff journalese one demands "What have you done for us lately?"

Dishing subtle dirt. Cheap talk. Black-and-white columns of Regardless in stark relief against particular: facades of Possible.

Newspapers don't kindle forest fires: news-makers do. Read between the lies. Everywhere-always. Coming to a lap-top near you.

Zealous Partners joined forever to the Nation — in limited liability — experiment with Futures. No-money-back: guaranteed.

It doesn't matter here-now this particular forever-day. They (you know: Them) don't care what you eat or if. So long as you believe in continental drift of Empire see to binding see: or profess such belief with vim-vigor enough to exact proud-grudge satisfaction.

Not easy as it looks to break the will of a people — however straight-jacketed and bound. Even upon receipt of custom-crucified cadaver (bullets sign-notarized by Authorized Personnel) the lucky winner demands more splash-effect: gut photographs of inside-out.

CAMERA PAN TO:

Dead eyes dead. Glossy glazed-donut dead: tender as the kid-gloves stuffed into your name: stamped "Penance."

Fool. Everybody knows damned well humor jokes wit rage impotence at: comic proxy cannon-shots at: situations you'll return to weekly — twenty minutes plus commercials till you're permitted to spend what remains of the night alone and stoned. Not your humor. Not your rage. What you really wanna do is go out and clobber someone-anyone in any way responsible for All This.

Way back in flower season: before the brothel: before diaper-rash from clammy sheets: the plaster-Paris Thinker — a site-marker for travelers — was removed from his customary position in the road. Seemed he had always been there: now he is gone.

This ongoing pursuit of adolescent night-thrills is a mistake. A huge mistake: hard to erase: it lingers: everywhere-always: like a dance tune played in all the clubs. Few notice it's there: fewer notice when it's gone.

Recall way back a convalescent scene of clammy sheets stained blood: the stiff on the gurney was you.

Night lingered. Some kind of...must be this huge mistake everywhere always like a popular tune.

Go ahead: pull my finger.

See? Even a fart draws nothing but blank stares.

Something's lacking: something essential: forgotten: hence difficult perhaps impossible to find much less renew.

Doctors goofing in surgery talk travel plans. Long vacations earned rummaging your innards for evidence: proof the operation was urgent and did indeed make sense and thousands of dollars all around how 'bout a cigar? Celebration of you: for you: over you: honoring you: despite you — may thy name and all it stood for — if anything — rest in penury and peace.

Children of our All

Lead us beyond frightening frightened boot-steps deep to real.

Lead us to Judges: Land Lords: Those Who Decide. Love's squalor and ideal betrayed by imitation fruit: pink-slip codicils to freedom (as possibility): as-if: "my kingdom: my kingdom" for a hearse: or Paradise for obscene visions: barren cities: sealed deposit boxes: stealthy footsteps: echo-clap of sandal-slap through corridors of shadow — centuries to come.

No vocabulary to describe the idiocy: the paper.

For instance: They can count you on their fingers: but won't bother: though this is the digital epoch of systemic spiders: fingers: creepy crawlers: eyes. Watch them crawl the creepy-creep across your kitchen floor. Giga-zooms of 010101010101010101010 over and under.

Now your head is meaningless.

They won't see you: They won't hear you: They're autistic: and They're in control. It's maddening I know: but it's the way of things: and They are All.

My what big guns you have. Is that battalion *really* yours?

They won't answer. They won't bother.

All the money in the world to Them is merely all the money in the world.

Enough to drive a thinking feeling breathing one insane: see what good *that* does. They'll walk through you: look through you: without knowing feeling smelling hearing sensing you: not the You in you at any rate.

They won't see you: They won't hear you: They're autistic: and They're in control. It's maddening I know: but it's the way of things: and They are All.

They don't know who They are themselves: why would They ever bother knowing you?

As Everybody knows: a finger is a finger is a rock a human tree. Aliens in soup-tureens light up the sky with rocket-blood: bark "Mac-attack!" at skyscrapers: genuflect to Baal. So what?

That toenail you won at the Fair and flushed days later — dead cause he ate like a *cochone* — was all your fault: you fed him skin.

Alligators in the sewer and the artichoke-banana-fig band playing "My-land of the Mine."

They won't see you: They won't hear you: They're autistic: and They're in control. It's maddening I know: but it's the way of things: and They are All.

You can't leave you know: Away is gone forever. Full Spectrum Dominance the only game in town. They own exclusive rights to the Past and all actions re-actions and emotions displayed and/or enacted therein: as well as memories: daydreams: epiphanies: hazy recollections — anything and everything associated with the aforementioned property.

Nothing is new under the sun: They've written every act and scene.

You're thinking: "I can reason with Them." Hoping maybe to appease? It's like that *Twilight Zone* when Li'l Opie wrecked the planet with his bad-seed mind. Wished to The Corn Field all fuss-budgets who disagreed with peanut-butter-hamburgers and ice-cream.

What's in The Cornfield you ask?

You don't wanna know.

They can't see you: They won't hear you: They're autistic: and They're in control. It's maddening I know: but it's the way of things: and They are All.

You don't want to think about anything because They know when you're not thinking Their desire. They know — and they don't like it. If you're not thinking Their desire whose desire are you thinking? More importantly: why? If you're not thinking Their desire maybe you HATE Them: maybe you want them GONE: maybe you don't want them back again: NEVER EVER NEVER. This upsets Them. They won't see or hear or count you but They want you to love Them: always — or be dead.

Love Them like you've never loved anyone ever: always — or be dead.

Of this we can be absolutely certain:

They won't see you: They won't hear you: They're autistic: and They're in control. It's maddening I know: but it's the way of things: and They are All.

Swaying Precarious

If Winter comes can Spring be far behind? — Shelley

Straight-jacketed and cuffed for mocking Death's assumption
of my mirror I was at liberty to choose: custom-crucifixion
or celebrity-autographed slug (hollow-point splash-effect
inside-out: cameras pan dead audience eyes: unthinkable).

Oh blessed mercy of The Crossed!

Holy-man said: "Tender thy name to God's gulag hand that
thou mayst kiss kid-gloves. Repent."

But surely Holy-man had known lubricious noons and
startling awake-nights drunk (throbbing: music: dance)?
Surely Holy-man — yes even he — had swayed precarious
over the booze-blank I-whole?

He said: "Pray. Pray. Supplicate. Cast away thine Righteous
Indignation of the Wronged. Pawn thine ass: idiot: and beg!
Else..."

All this mass to from. It almost feels.

"Tell me: Holy-man" I said. "If Winter comes: can Spring
up from behind and beat you senseless: pocket yer heart
and scram — but anyway: no harm done? Or blast infinities
through multi-cell orgasmic merge of womb with stretched
pursuit of matter-deep Abstraction's yearning far? Extend
your go-Me trips to radical-immerse with Other?

"Will She blow minds senseless? Will She wear soft clothes?"

Holy-man muttered "Hopeless. Hopeless."

Silently I asked — not prayed to any god: and certainly not to
save my sorry ass — for Quagmire Sue's ascent.

Oh Quagmire Sue! Will your country-root-rock-band
survive the ladder-climb — or set folks blue? Open money-
flood conduits to Happy — or yield imperatives to segment-

think: fickle Market-requisitions of Consume?

Will you still blast life-surround decibels in Freedom-mode: perform raucous gigs — stalwart: sidereal: immense — to tend the anyways of Life: no broke to mend? Will devote-to-amuse kill genius-of-explore?

Once: clock-watched job-minutes flushed errant avenues till Friday Night's eternity-trip to unexplored endorphine-zones. Two hours in Sacred Time you mesmerized *der Volk* — and me too: then.

Now you are Huge. Do not annihilate us when you peak: Sue: please: do not annihilate yourself with drink.

Holy-man closed The Book and scowled.

"I condemn ye to thy dark reward" he shrugged. "May god have mercy on your soul."

"Piss off Holy-man" said I — what'd I have to lose? "A pox on yer god: and his little dog: Two! I'll see that dark reward and raise you seven life-times of Eternal Spring. God can play too if he's game. So long as he ante's up. No pay no play."

Eternal We Contemplate

In memory-flush of neural circuit transient nothings to behold.

We know too much how little we really know of what we know. The necessity of keeping one's True intact: that is: not lose oneself to spectacular befuddlements like Knowing sun-moon-stars as object-spectacles: debris: fetid waste of day-month-years digested and disbursed so long long long ago.

The Eternal we contemplate — so far away from our green chairs — the We we believe is in us yet not Us. We know what we think we know because what we know we learned from books written by Those Who Know. What is known to Those Who Know are faces from Africa: Mexico: Egypt: timeless in our dreams. Those Who Know explain to us that our dreams are not our selves: that we ourselves are not even our selves: we're minerals: chemicals: electric currents. What a bummer. How sad. Though on the bright side: our selves are not Eternal. Been a long run: but the show's gotta end. Sooner or later.

The Ones Who Know pursue and catch us always. One can't blame them: how else would they sell their pills? Sooner or later — after much expensive R&D — They'll find out exactly what we are and — cruel vindictive bastards — tell us.

Don't misunderstand. I believe. I believe the pills create or simulate some form of Happy. I merely suggest perhaps depression would not be so damned bad if we had at least some notion of ourselves as Ourselves and not whatever it is they'll ultimately find out we've become. When they've accumulated: studied: interpreted and peer-reviewed all relevant data.

Surely it was better to believe that to be human was to be like-god. And when we killed god that was fine too: for we became better than like-god: we became god.

And don't blame Darwin for this: he merely noticed patterns: like Karl Marx. Of adaptability and change. And wasn't it good that while once we were less than what we are we evolved to become more?

But now it doesn't matter: really: whether we are less or more or become better than the more we are at present: for it can all be broken down to formulas equations code and what not: and indexed.

For instance: First Love: those radiant memories we cherished. Chemical-stimulants. Hormones amplifying sublimations of sensation in our blah blah blah bleh bleh beh in loco *loco pubis orgasmus* flagrantly *delictoed* and so on so forth.

We drove a nice car to the restaurant at dusk. Later in the back-seat: sweat-embrace of passion and perfume. Now: decades later: Love is not experience we owned. From whatever perspective it is recalled — or whose.

Human all too Human pulse through synapse-wire stimulates our thing-a-ma-jigs: turns awkward balcony-scene to urgent sex-farce emblazoned by Imagination before passed on to Memory like table-salt or napkins. Memory whose lurid adjectives provoked the whole myth-take of synapse as Romance.

Yearn: yearn: yearn: amounts to nothing.

Eon-pain endure of quashed desire: minds snuffed on a thousand killing fields and talk-shows. Can even our Others be significant if there's no there there: or here: or anywhere else?

Yes: the lovers: all of them: from fumbling first-crush to One-and-Only-Truly. Complex systems interact: compendium of mortal stuff. Generates heat.

We wander Epic Systems: establishment our totem tree. How we march through day-to-day days without choking or puking is mysterious: one of the few mysteries left to us Good Country People who live instructed by cemetery narratives about what we cherish: what we believe: what we were told and expected to believe and cherish: what we were told to know we believe is good and sacred: and what we are expected to know for damned shit-sure is not.

We seem sad and disappointed but we are not really because WE ARE NOT: really. There are ones who can prove this and ultimately will — following proper research — and publish it as fact and make us curse their names for stranding us between two worlds: that of the spirited sensual Who and the sensational but senseless What.

Though ultimately and in truth: I see no reason to probe deep the what-why-wherefore of It All so close to extinction of both Pain and Pleasure. Might as well pursue the latter and avoid the former however I can: as much as I can: for as long as I can.

Prescription States

During ostensible... when rights... before they bombed better than ourselves for lesser crimes than outrage: loathing: disgust. Too long now going-too-far has gone too far: too long now it's been too late to pursue Become.

"... relax it's just another generation: it'll pass: they all grow old so quick... "

It is the moral fashion of our time to be lifeless: shit-less: sex-less: diseased creatures — beasts is far too elegant a word.

"What is is what is: like: you know? Anyway: a new Election's coming. They promised us peanut-butter. And Freedom. Or was it peanuts and free butter? Either way they're both the lesser of two evils."

This seems strange and low. But then: we are sick.

As long as prescription states marshal us through steely freeze of never-days (our breath smells of synthetic mint) we will never be as angry as we are afraid. And anxious for renewal of our pills. Prescriptions are not guaranteed: all — even our own — are subject to review.

Tin-canned laughter of drug-pushers: usurpers: zealots: punctuate the Cultural Discourse. And slick ads for anti-anxiety-anti-depressant boosters: ask your primary care physician or local recruiter about the Communal Action Process Employment Unity Plan (CASE UP) legislation. They'll tell you all about education: emotional maturity: a killer-resume employers can't refuse: and other benefits of swapping two years' patriotic service for partial tuition-remission (after taxes).

No education in legs blown off a million lives from home till after class. A day late a gimp. Lessons-learned sequestered deep require deep-psyche introspection: puffing e-lectronic cigarettes alone in a dark room.

... user-friendly taste real good in a variety of strengths

nothing but nicotine real tobacco flavoring and water don't wake up feeling you've sucked the fart out of a Volkswagon brighten your mornings with the cheaper healthier...

...brothers blown apart blood scalds your skin. Movies music television sound-and-fury of idiots bored.

Anticipate thunder in dry colonies...

Voice in the Night

What is the nature of your pain? You do not "fit in" it seems. Does this upset you? You say you want a revolution but despise the sight of blood. How can this possibly make sense?

I thought it was just a Life thing: you know: a matter of determine: fit to scale. The wall of human separates: Desire from Achieve and all that.

Faith propels Forever — beyond blasted years of folks like you — toward some Someday: the Past and all the rest to flotsam-jetsam overboard.

I am a deliberate animal: struggling: perturbed. Yes I am mindful of the great As-If: as-if Possible floats on lifeless sexless diseased What Is. Striving adrift the sea of consequence.

Think: mind over matter. Meditate upon it man think hard.

Matter doesn't matter anymore.

Well: really: that's relative.

Relative to what?

Your miserable lump of human-be.

So: what then?

How should I know? I'm not a god. I'm just a voice from the depths: of you no less. In other words: not all that deep.

How deep? How Me? More of Me or less of Me than me? What I believe I am.

DNA-deep. What is Language — or it's cheap toy: Belief? Abstractions of your own substantial.

What about my thoughts? I mean My thoughts?

"In the beginning was the word." Language is generic thought: idiot. You think your ideas — so-called — are your own?

My thoughts: my mind.

Don't tell me you fell for that old linguistic burp. Didn't they use that or some such "freedom to be original" nonsense to sell computers or motorcycles way back when? Forgot the name of the Ad-Man who conceived it.

Whose — if not mine?

Think of how many minds how many centuries "your" words passed through during their etymological travels before passing — briefly — through yours over the course of Human-Be. Not all that long: but thousands of times the sum-total of your You.

I still have time.

Not much. That's part of the gag. A human life-time is never long enough to develop an actual character beyond whatever experiences one or another individual selects from all that he/ she has experienced: according to one's inherited predilection for this or that "personality."

But there is a Me: that is: the essence of me: the —

Soul?

Well: no. But who or whatever decides which experiences I choose to define as me: That's Me.

Nope. That's not you: that's Me.

Well that is a gag. Playing practically a joke. What's the other part? Of the gag I mean.

You'll find out.

I'm impatient. I don't like surprises.

Nobody does. That's why you're all a bunch of control freaks:

religious zealots: litigators: and what not.

Give me a hint.

I'll do better. I'll give you a quote: "Life is but a fart blown through the winds of existence. Briefly."

Lovely. Who the hell said that?

You did. Or maybe it was Me. I can't recall. No matter: it's nothing new or original. It can't be. It cannot possibly be.

What is this nothing-new-under-the-sun type crap you're feeding me? Talk about clichés. No one ever has any original ideas?

I didn't say that. At best it's a collaboration.

Alright: how about this? "Occasionally some One is right about some Thing: but Everyone is Always wrong about Everything."

Cute: but no cigar. Your "some One" usually just says what Everyone already knows: or has at least pondered enough to reach a possible but most unwelcome conclusion. Hence: they back away.

Goddamn it. Look at me: I'm haunted.

Yeah: so?

So do something. Don't tell me all this crap is "in the DNA."

Why not? Nature never fucks-up? Why do you think so many species go extinct — not counting the ones humanity knocked-off?

Okay okay okay okay. Yeah: yeah. Sure: sure. I'm not gonna just sit here like a duck and wait. I mean: every problem has a solution: right?

Yeah. Sure. Have Faith. Whatever. Hopeless.

Come on man. For a Voice from the Depths you're pretty shallow. This is ridiculous. Absurd. That's all you got stored in that double-helix alphabet it took god or the cosmos or nature or whatever a million years to construct? You gotta give me something.

You are in fact way more Me than you are You: so there's not much more I can say about "what the definition of 'is' is."

Do me a solid will ya?

I'll do unto you what you tried to pull over on me. I'll give you a quote.

Eager to hear it. My ears are open and my mouth is shut.

For a change. Okay: here goes: "As the billy-goat dashed madly through the boulevard bleating to be killed."

As the billy-goat dashed and bleated. What? What?

Figure it out. Ciao.

Music Loud Sing Dance To

History its histories of full great good perpetuations. History is hard upon its millions: billions: particularly its ones. Hiroshima dropped on Tokyo unleashed the power of a thousand suns. So many Before-and-Afters blown to ash.

The Revolution of Loud Sing Dance To music was forbidden to poets who hypnotized old men in coffee-bars — poor codgers arched like question marks over their newspapers: happy to stroke their beards and be left the Hell alone.

Anyway: The Revolution changed everything — as it relates to song and dance.

The New Republic — still forbidden to versifiers so that venerable coots can read clear muscular prose in peace — allows some universities to teach Sing-Dance music played loud so long as pedagogues are expert and discreet. Sing-Dance music played loud can provoke unstable reactions. Naive undergraduates rise to dance and sing: loud: louder than airplanes: louder than bombs: louder — if can be imagined — than Sousa-drones of political discourse.

Public records indicate records are demanded by the Public — as such media exist in modern digital format. Sounds disseminated create opportunities: increase desire for possession so far as such intangibles as sound can be possessed. In fairness: the ability to summon sounds at will: pause: rewind: replay — provided proper hard and soft ware are available — does indicate some manner of keeping: having: own.

Business advertising business can therefore be improved and amplified by whatever siren songs will most likely seduce consumers to this fickle market.

The music-energy required to arouse aforementioned consumers is low — relative to fads and formulas of their forbears. Nevertheless: when talented musicians play consumers dance from drinks till dawn.

Such power must be harnessed. The Revolution must promote and manufacture sounds the Public yearns to hear. Taste is unpredictable: familiarity with histories of past successes — and failures — virtually meaningless.

"Beat heart be hard" is one general demand.

"Music Loud Sing-Dance To" is another.

Who can tell? The Revolution is young: still a-blush with morning's glow. History its histories. Great good options exist millions: billions: ones. Hiroshima dropped on Tokyo. Convention blown to ash.

Wounds Received

Let me tell you friends about the Big Team work force. Soldiers home for din-din. Our boys returned at last from the exotic Death March with yarns to spin and chains to pull. Tales of adventure sure to thrill the kids: stymie uncles who've seen-it-all (but lust for more): enthrall grim neighbors and wayward aunts: befuddle all manner of fussbudgets and ironic passers-by. Home-Coming to *der Homeland*. The last-stop. End of tour.

Mass to from. It almost feels.

May the dance macabre commence! Do the "Quick Jitters:" the "Sleepless:" the "Get-to-bar" and "Pick-up-six!"

Splendid shenanigans are guaranteed for all: rompers stompers hoofers even dance-challenged wall-flowers (disabled). So make with the hootenanny — you'll stomp these steps and more: or get drunk and pretend!

Black Suits optional.

Soldiers: forget your addictions: heed not cravings for "one more kick:" a true hero knows when to — no: I will not lie. There is no greater thrill than *that*. Thus: the road to job security is a job in Security. License to carry though not — not always — use.

Do not: I repeat: do not sink. Emerge from the booze-blank I-whole. Rise! But lay low...

Courage: fortitude: patience. Consider martyrs. Consider Man in the Black Suit: cipher *extraordinaire*: inventor of The Code: ingenious Alpha Bet of nothing-signified. Fully encrypted in Black Suit.

The pass-phrase to whisper when Black Suit passed — "Hey: what's with that guy?" — was created — the theory goes — to foster independent processes of ultimate recourse. Keep rhythm while marching to civilian drums. Sounds better — what I am saying — with repetition. Our common mantra will glue us back from fragments: disparate and dispersed as they are: as we are: during these days of decompression Oh-So-Stressful on us all.

It is indeed obscene to watch the ink drip. Vile pages of journals we are required to submit for perusal until we are safely out of what They — our Masters — deem the Addiction-Zone. A question of Mental Health: objectively determined and defined.

Consider again the endurance of Man in the Black Suit: of whom the rabble whisper: "It's not a job he goes to... it's a hospital!"

For wounds received: for surgeries: for faces and personae shattered ages ago and reconstructed. Still: yet: again.

Man in the Black Suit can barely speak: so addled is he now: so mesmerized by Their synthetic drugs and images: Their subtle Time-corruptions.

He says repeatedly the same-old same-again-same:

"The the. Not good for. The the. The war. I mean. Away: away. That is: it's all just ink. I am. Just ink."

Diary of a Drab-man

Dear Diary:

Nothing much happened today in the great wide world. Folks got whacked someplace far away I forget the name there were a bunch of places. Who can tell what's where with all those people always blowing up cars because this or that god told 'em to? Heathens. If they'd just turned Christian like the missionaries told'em a thousand years ago they wouldn't be in this mess.

Also: some kind of fighting broke out or "situation deteriorated" as the news-guy said: in — where else? — Iraq. Serves 'em right for... uh... what was it? Something about Saddam threw a donut or a sponge-cake — yeah: that's it: it was a yellow cake — at Colin Powell in the middle of a UN meeting. But that was like a million years ago and they still won't quiet down.

Whatever.

All I know is that Saddam guy looked a helluva lot like Adolf Hitler. Well: not in actual face or body type. But he did have a mustache and those beady eyes Hitler had. Also: the Russians are at it again — some things never change — messing up our freedom fighters in the Ukraine. The shit hasn't hit the fan yet: but it's staring hard with angry eyes...

Meanwhile: Network Video finally sent me that movie *Decline of All* and the god-damned disk was cracked I couldn't play it. Can you believe that shit? Second time that happened to me. I should just straight-out stream or download over the Network. Also: as I suspected: that e-cigarette/vaporizer I ordered works only for nicotine. You need a special kind of battery and a thingamajig to vaporize hash and get any kind of buzz off it. Real bummer. I don't have real hash: but I found out how to make a kind of hash-like goo from soaking herb in grain alcohol and letting it evaporate. I spent a lot of time on this batch and was looking forward to vaping with my Sweet Petunia this week-end.

Speaking of which: my Sweet Petunia found out who it was went murdering and dismembering all those six-year-old kids around the neighborhood before it was even on the news — I don't have a kid: just my dog: Alphie: but imagine if some maniac slit his throat and dismembered and disemboweled poor Alphie!

The brutal psycho-killer maniac was none other than my Sweet Petunia's twelve-year-old daughter: Laura-Beth. Really freaked me out.

I always kinda liked that kid. Strange about her doing stuff to squirrels and cats around the neighborhood: but it really wasn't my place to say. So long as she swore she'd keep her meat-hooks — literally — off Alphie: which she did swear.

"So" I said to Sweet Petunia. "What're you gonna do? "

"Let her stew in there — some kind of holding cell or something — and think good and hard about what she did and what kind of punishment she thinks she deserves for getting caught."

"Tough love. But it's the right thing to do. Honestly: she's almost a teenager: she can't just off a bunch of pre-schoolers without raising a fuss."

"Exactly. Then of course I'll have to get her a lawyer. Got a call from that hot-shot attorney who gets kids off on the Adderall defense."

"What: these kids are so stoked on speed they don't know what they're doing?"

"No: the opposite. I had a script from her pediatrician. She wasn't abusing the stuff or anything: but when I called all my main connections — Walgreens: Duane Reade: Rite Aid: CVS — to make sure they had generic Adderall so I could score as quickly and conveniently as possible — they're just plain amphetamine salts really — they all told me the same thing: they cannot divulge that information over the phone. What the fuck? So I had to run all over town going from place to place and of course every pharmacy was out of stock — you know how that stuff flies off the shelves. Especially during final-exam time."

"Oh. I get it. She needed her medically prescribed medication: but because of some law or insurance thing poor Laura-Beth was cut off cold. Of course she went over-the-top with pent-up rage: withdrawal: whatever."

"Yup."

"Anything else?"

"Nope. Kinda boring day: all things considered. You?"

"Same. We might have to smoke not vape this week-end. I ordered the wrong gadget."

"Told you. Well: no matter. So long as we can smoke a bit: chill out: watch the movie."

I was gonna break the news about the movie but figured it could wait till she was less stressed-out...

I guess that's all for today.

Hope tomorrow something happens. Not to me: of course. But really I'm so damned bored I wanna see some kind of action: know what I mean?

Opium on the Beach with Cuban

Preface: (Maduro: long thick dark as a horse's —)

Part I

White hot beaches of our cunning sea ocean my tongue: not fish: complexity marked Tincture of You: liquid womb-life: lubricant: *ichor*. Salty summer hair. Thighs clenched wet and muscular beneath a vinyl beach umbrella (ocean my tongue) and you.

Part II

I'm serious: no laughing now: I'm... ambidextrous?

The End

Author's Statement:

I'm a Sudden Novelist (not — as some wag remarked — "suddenly a novelist"). I write tall tales in less than half a page — the focus-group approved norm for Sudden Fiction. I stretch the truth only so far as required by The Conglomerate's Manual of Style and General Guidelines (COMANGEN).

I write about myself and minor goings-on: not anything dealing with world events or the Empire's international engagements.

Okay: so we Free People can't get real opium or laudanum cause it's more profitable to synthesize the stuff into oxycodone: fentanyl: morphine sulfate: etc. But I did indeed go to the beach with my prescription bottle of Big Pharma's time-release goof-balls. Because real Cubans — both cigars and people — are illegal I vaped-up my favorite Cigar (*e-Romeo e-Julietta*: 8-hour battery life guaranteed no ashes) and had me a good long smoke — or vape.

Aw hell: gimme a break.

According to my agent Curt Clipp: Book-O-Rama plans not only to turn *Opium on the Beach* into a feature film and feature me on the Network Book Club channel: but an appearance of yours truly on the cover of several major magazines (hard-copy and Networked) is rumored to be a hypothetical possibility: almost certain.

subject to yeah

I was subject to Yeah for willing sounds stray: a bit too far left or perhaps right of Standard Trend-Origin Music Protocol (STOMP) than even the liberal interpreter can silently suffer: they must sing.

Idiots wanted — proverbial want-ads read. Sons of suffering to be put through worse. Qualified applicants assume Marketable positions. Bite. Hard. Bite that bullet hard son bite it hard.

"Can't you see that? Can't you open your eyes for one god-damned minute and just see that? Or at least see something if not 'that' specifically?"

She repeated this throughout the night: but I couldn't figure out exactly what "that" she was referring to: much less anything else. Or something else: as she apparently preferred.

Years of this can alter: displace: even obliterate — zap poof gone — one's ability to feel.

Babel Plugged

After his last disastrous gig The Inventor (architect-engineer-patent-holder of Pandora's Box — liability pending claim his attorneys) sought solitude: silence: peace.

His next project — The Library of Babel — was at the very least critically accepted. Borges himself sent The Inventor a share of royalties from the eponymous "Library of Babel" in several translations — though revenue from even an anthologized short-story can't compare to the double-helices of data dense within and surging out from the Library of Babel!

He needed something.

"I need something" The Inventor lamented. "Some thing. Gee: but what?"

Again The Inventor sequestered himself and again his efforts bore fruit: big fruit: bigger than god's —

"This is a thing. This is a big thing" The Inventor dictated to his box. "Scratch that. This is a huge world-shaking mega-monster giggly-goodly god-damned thing!"

He bowed to standing ovations of audiences who would soon not be imaginary.

"All you gotta do" he began but checked himself to get a grip: hold back giggles: dry tears. He continued: "All you gotta do...all you gotta do is plug the Library of Babel into a fucking wall!"

The dam burst: a roaring flood of giggles: chortles: snickering guffaws.

And so The Inventor sparked galaxies of screens with knowledge: entertainment: social networks: political journals: blogs: 24/7 extremist rants and cute cuddly animals with "Cheer up enjoy your day!" messages available in every available language and format on All Media Conglomerate

(ALMCON) Network's Portal for News Comedy Music Idol Sports and lots and lots of quality pornography.

The Inventor brought all the world's knowledge (but very little wisdom) to the User's fingertips.

(NOTE: all data from the Library's infinite collection is selected: dispersed: and reviewed at User's own risk. Genius Inventor Inc. assumes no liability for poor judgment).

Yet again the Inventor found himself alone and tortured: haunted — albeit in a much much bigger house. Tortured by genius? Or haunted by gut-core nausea of remorse erupting from a well-intentioned notion turned colossal fuck-up?

Evidence Fades with Comet Intent

A Comet emerges from the cold black Greater Than. Experts predict this massive harbinger of sudden-impact-doom will punch out Gaea's lights sometime in June 2085. I read this notion on a Science site of excellent repute (though: so many volumes known and unknown in this Library of Babel: who can distinguish between Reputable and Deranged?)

"Why must you kick me down grasping?" she cried. "You promised peanut butter and chocolate cream cheese. And chill-hugs — better than nothing."

"Oh: please. I've never laid a hand or foot on you and never would. Ok? Hush."

She settled: briefly: struck a lower pose.

The article said this Comet is large: fast: and was discovered close — relative to light-year measurements and what-not. The Comet carries a kind of steadfast certainty that contrasts sharply with standard calculations of random risk (performed on Super-Computers by Experts at The University).

This cosmic flake of ice dust is apparently "streaming the upper fuzz course limits of strike orbit" and similar scientific cockle-doodle-do. So much jargon-jargon tossed like boiling oil over the parapets of Ivory Tower.

Nevertheless: the words "Giga-ton collision estimate" struck hard.

She said: "Night-terror. Dream-fighting exhausts potential: distance I mean: the physical."

"What? What?"

She said: "This fucking sucks."

It's just a giant snow-ball really: and calculations of distant space-objects newly discovered are premature at best. But those astronomers mean business. The Comet will be punctual if not fully precise: it is expected to strike on time: more or less. Direct line of impact. Year 2085 is not exactly Tomorrow: but still.

"My land-lord's mom died" she said. "Just telling you."

Who can cope with these absurd demands? Courage and strength wither: the Mind becomes a storm of turmoil: panic-disarray: discomfort. And it's not like anyone will help or "deliver us:" divert the Dark-Eternal via sharp-angle degree-twist of the Comet's course...

Such scenarios can be stressful.

"Give me art and send me dick" she snapped. "Shits and giggles. Crap a better hurt today?"

All this uncertainty. "Exact out-gassing is slim" say professional sky-gazers. "One in 120 million dealing tails" or something. They really should have some kind of lay interpreter: a regular idiot who speaks to be heard and understood. Darkness expounds upon darkness: arcane equations "clarify" unto the umpteenth power of perplexity.

The overall message is clear: many centuries of accumulation will be forcefully removed. No second acts or evolution of another species or anything like that I don't think. Absence: silence: particles: gas: dust. Shapeless. Blah.

She said: "God-damned Hannibal Lecter sadist! You offer nothing: shame a la carte and a side of vomit. All is lost on you always: you arrogant prick!"

I imagine there'll be heaps of publicity in 2084 — possibly sooner. Casinos run amok. Bet the house: what can you lose? Perhaps Science will develop a Comet-smasher. Repel the ice with fire or lasers or some such Big Plan stuff the media will hype as Operation Comet Intent.

"Grief. Sadness. Tender death" she mumbled: a heap of nothing on the rug. "You distort me."

Some things not even hot-shot Scientists are able to predict. Regardless: evidence fades. Eventually.

The Process

It's hard to believe another day could end this way. That we won't finally — after all — wake up. Just-a-dream and all that.

Honestly: I never imagined it would come so — not sudden: it was a sequence of degeneracies: noticeable in sum: but hard to detect during the slow-slide-down.

Never imagined it would come so run-of-the-mill. The process I mean. Not the thing itself: which cannot possibly exist. You can be living: you can't be dead. Well: relative to others around you: sure: you can be dead: as in "he was alive: now he is dead." But after an eon or two: when it's all stone underground and dust and no one is around except Walt Disney-type freaks who had themselves mummified or freeze-dried or what-not no one is really dead: not to the living. They simply do not exist: and never existed at all: unless referenced in some fossil text. Of course: if they did thaw-out old Walt and juice him up with years he'd be alive: not dead. For a while.

Death is an end not a state. I hope. I hate all this All This. It was all so very different before the Process: before the crumbling: when I was out there: you know: out there in the life. This is not death: it's being dead. Most of it — the long Before and all-too-sudden After. The first descent was part of being dead: among others who were dead: like my room-mates — the Processed — were part of dead.

I'm half naked: gown won't tie.

Cold steel invasions: tubes: catheters: embarrassing baths: over-head television 24/7 (and this is the good nightmare: the one with health insurance).

Still believe in Future as a pretense: like Humanity or Democrats: belief for belief's sake: so they don't call you Nihilist or Gloomy Gus. So iffy really: unreliable: so not like we were taught.

It's all conducted with Middle-Management-indifference.

As we the Processed lay listless: bored: dispirited: grim.

Regardless of despair (bottomless): or faith (half-assed): or false good cheer: regardless of the utter fictions we lose ourselves to between pills and War Stories of meaningless suffering: we cling to that old fairy tale drummed into us all of us — by Mama: Grandma: Sister Sue — that we are special: unique: wonderful as life: we are miraculous. And all of that.

"We're good people" we tell ourselves. "We're worthy of life because we were born."

And of course the Girls who clean our pans and ride the bus — alone: past midnight — really do love us and think about us (alone: past midnight) and want us to get well. Of course.

Even when we cover our eyes: put our hands to our ears: scream "Yonk! Yonk! Yonk!" it comes: it comes: regardless of our fear: the Process comes when we are forced awake from three maximum four hours sleep by whatever aide or intern on duty demands blood or piss or scrapes for live cells.

It persists: and we persist: until we do not.

Bomb is God

The gun and the typewriter: mechanical genius of The Nation: yes: but Bomb is god. Ur-Bomb and its technological descendants.

Religions reign until meaner more powerful nations overtake them — State and Belief being one — and supplant the conquered deities with their own gods — obviously more powerful cause they won: duh: end of topic.

But not the end if we consider what or rather Who became the dominant god of the dominant religions of the dominant empires and nations: the gods as one god with attributes that seem — in dreaming and psychotic eyes — peculiarly like those of a person. God the all-knowing-seeing creator of all things known unknown and unfathomable could not appear unto his children as he was lest he blow their mortal minds: hence: the universal mind-sculpt fictionalized itself as One the people might relate to: a hugely powerful and scary yet unseen untouchable amalgam of the everything and all: the great I AM that I AM: slogan blood and marrow of eternal corporate person-hood.

Men hate and fear The Corporation: just as they hated and feared the omnipotent omniscient fickle jealous capricious and downright scary One-God-or-Else.

So the nation-state or empire with the baddest god wins. God is Bomb: and related contraptions. One Nation under Bomb with liberty and justice for all: indivisible under spangled flags of Death.

It ain't rocket-science: though rocket-science is integral to Bomb.

Naked

During the initial stupor (inevitable by-product of captivity) I studied my body in the mirror: naked: naked as the day I was born — the first time: the birth I hadn't chosen by myself for myself of myself: by-of-for some body's Self: ultimately. More or less.

I hated the sight of that thing. Humiliation of meat and form: body of ugliness. Thought I'd done with all that long ago.

I smashed the glass.

Once: I believed I was a sort of phantom (The Phantom I indeed did call myself) sailing through bodies in which lives occurred — briefly — before disappeared-to-dust: then on I'd go to a new life's body: again and again and again over the course of centuries.

But all the bodies I'd fled had been my own: characters and personalities I'd lived over the course of years — not centuries — like everyone else. Only one body had occurred: it has yet to disappear.

They — my Keepers — replaced the mirror.

I requested darkness. And — if they would not mind — a small light under which to read the words I type. On paper no less. What place is this? What century?

They provided me with one of those small lamps travelers and commuters clip to books and brief-cases in order to maximize efficiency of Down-Time lost to perpetual motion — planes: trains: buses. Time = Money: pages accumulate. I'd actually thought books had been superannuated long ago: replaced by those thing-a-ma-jigs that serve as phone-entertainment-center what-not all-in-one Solutions.

But again: I'm not aware — as I haven't been appraised by my Keepers — of time or place — day: night: week: month: century — just supplied with paper: a sheaf for typing and a roll to wipe my ass — yet another grotesque function of form.   And my little chair and table. And cot. And a new glass abyss in which to gaze deep at whoever bothers to gaze back. So I peck away at this antique type-writer mechanism: in darkness.

He who dares peruse these prophesies beware: The Typos are a-commin' — and they mean Business...

Not quite darkness. I have my little book-light. Clipped to my proboscis. Pain: a pinch. Another post-it-note reminder of my status. Fine and well. Dandy. Keeps me awake. Bodies must sleep: but sleep brings dreams of freedom: ubiquity: immanence: eternal being of The Phantom — not this stark meat nothing-lump of human-be.

Actually: from what I've seen — briefly — it's not a bad body as bodies go: but all bodies must go: and should.

Note: Time is not money. Money — like Law — is just a human notion. Time is Time: like Space: an Absolute. Let's get our facts straight: delineate boundaries: especially in terms of Absolute: regardless of what one's definition of Is is.

Well. Well. Irrespective of in-any-case and not-withstanding: here I am. Another tour of duty in this mortal coil. Another incarnation. Been there: done that. Perhaps I can transform myself: or recreate myself. Escape this cell and the amalgam of cells within via the type-writer machine. Spit my spirit like a gob of spunk onto the page (forgot about that briefly pleasurable but ultimately messy-wet-disgusting   body function). The *little death*. Mind out of matter. But the page is also... matter? No matter. Keeps me occupied. Prevents me from — quells the sick but persistent temptation to flick on the light: stand before the mirror-abyss-glass-indictment of All This: and stare ("look upon these works: ye mighty: and despair...").

I can't help but notice that after a certain number of hours — how many: I could not possibly know — after I've finally succumbed to this ridiculously inefficient form's requirement for sleep I wake to find a virgin page placed neatly: lewdly: spread-eagle-wide-open juiced and ready — carriage-return cocked — in the typewriter: the words I'd written the day or night previous to sleep gone. Vanished. Poof.

Someone — who? my Keepers? their paramours? *other* prisoners? covert menials? — stealthily removes the bucket this body fills regularly with noxious excretions. When the body is asleep. Are there other prisoners? Is this a prison at all? Or am I alone with my Keepers — this cell a converted storage-closet in an otherwise expansive castle?

"To my Keepers:

"'Do I dare to eat a peach' — or throw it at your heads?

"Someone is reading these rants of mine. Or wiping their asses with them. If the former: I most humbly beseech you servants of my Keepers — or my Keepers themselves? — to send me water. Not the bottle of tepid stuff I sip throughout the day (night?). Hot water: and soap. Or perhaps a guide and guard might lead me out of here — blind-folded if necessary — toward a bath or shower-like facility. At the very least send incense. I hazard to guess that you too are in possession of a form (do we possess our forms: or do these cumbersome bags of meat-bone-stuff possess us?) and you are at least somewhat familiar with the phenomenon of an unwashed body that has marinated in its own excretions more than a few days running: they smell.

"Your humble meat-puppet: formerly known as...

"*The Phantom*"

Spinning void of spinning void. Nothing: no belief but spin. Nothing spinning nothingness from nothing. No wheels no cycles of recurrence. Nor god nor future: nor *pyrne* nor *gyre*.

No more: no more: no more moot-antiquated-and-irrelevant artifacts of Dream.

No fun to be corporate. Personified. Alone. No how nor why of *It* if can't-go-on-must-go-on goes on too long. Forever. Seemingly. And a day.

Penal code: Life = Eternity. Let Life = Life + 1: or for brevity and convenience: Life++

Nothing is certain: regardless of probable. I will leave this place. Possibly.

Once: I had a kind of life. I don't remember when. Hysterical exterior: interior a scream. Dusk descends from red to strange. You can't depend on night: the moon is not completely full: not always. Stars are relatively stable.

As ever (and ever and ever) yours:

The Phantom

The Ad-Man

He fed us vegetables and plant proteins — organically grown.

A moat of lawn and shrubbery distinguished his acres. Neighboring properties seemed less masterfully alive: as if even the green of their chlorophyll was artificial: diluted: second-rate.

Posters lined his walls: classic ad-campaigns through which he'd stoked the lusts of generations. Posters everywhere.

We smiled — inwardly — at memories of advertisements buried like nursery rhymes within us: primordial and inextricable.

The Ad-Man sculpted minds to desire what needed to be owned (according to the particular Client's base brand-leverage and product-awareness ratios: respectively).

True: he stirred — even among ourselves — unnecessary dream-conflicts: misguided longings. But only for certain must-move products — most long-forgotten.

Not forgotten were his images: his shimmering shibboleths and catchy tunes. His barbed one-liners penetrated deep: near-impossible to remove.

"I did not create the desires of men and women: I steered painful energies toward palpable-attainable" the Ad-Man said.

"The people want: it is their nature. They need The Ad-man to tell them what to want and how desperately: to tell them what will satisfy: to teach them to look deep within themselves and see my point: refine their tastes: from each according to his assets to each according to his wares.

"The Ad-Man aims not to please but to enlighten. So that hungers one can never satisfy might in the best of circumstances be appeased.

"I believe exhausted objects will return: eventually. They will be craved: again.

"The Ad-Man persuades the people to choose wisely: the only unwise choice is Nothing.

"Everyone: please: eat a little: drink up: the night is young — as are you all..."

He showed us his prizes: honorary degrees: mementos of a life lived conjuring innovative fancies. It was he — The Ad-Man — one of his plaques proclaimed — who had created Illusion of Essential: who managed to invoke — like none before or since — the essence of Yearn: who mastered feral dithyrambs of satisfaction-guaranteed (deferred-till-purchase) like a skilled: motivated: dominant lover.

Much — so very much — is owed. An enormous debt...

Focus

Beyond belief in numinous noise-borders — camouflaged — crystalline spectra spawn fervid processes of shade.

The truth is intricate as chip-set thoughts: rare as pearls in mud: valuable as Elvis

ground to powder scattered: seeding money-orchards: diamonds in pears.

So long as the Market endures your paper daydreams shall endure

the Market.

But there's a Catch: bitter clown — so sentimental for the sound of music (closets overflowing soundtrack DVDs)!

To endure the Market is to wander deserts of youth's dream-time: pitch cacophony in heat-bloat-stink of mid-life's reckoning: believe beyond mere proof-of-purchase that backseat love-islands of Billy Holiday and Jimmy Dean are null: void: barren — no ghosts: no trace-elements of blood or semen — and know it is the god-damned truth that random moments sequentially lived are the real realities that Real is: not Memory lying again: as it was ever ruthless-and-relentless wont to do.

In fact: whatever confusion one might have experienced was not random at all: but The Good Old Days logistically determined to the last detail: complete with music and design — meaningful and purposeful — to bring you to the Now now.

So get a grip: focus.

Be confident that Future is indeed what *must be* despite odd-various annoyances within the scheme. Must it begin again and play in similar fashion to The End — this controlled experiment in disarray?

Forget such tripe. Know the Market of the Real.

Fifty years gone: fifty years!   And still I ask you: seriously: still: yet: again: and still-yet-again expect an honest answer:

When oh when oh when will you *finally* marry Peggy Sue?

The Patient Lies Etherized Upon the Table

Let him be. Give him a cigarette if he comes to. So he's
dying of lung-cancer: so what? It's a terminal case. Dose
him with morphine whenever he asks: whether for analgesic
or recreational redress.

I know: I know: "We're gonna do something: something
serious and huge: we're gonna fix stuff."

No yer not. You're just gonna talk about stuff on that thar
Information-overloaded sub-prime highway cluttered with
Road Pizza: broken hearts: and discarded bottles under
perpetual noon-blaze of Surveillance.

Everything you say — and write — will be held against
you. Not that it matters. What are They (you know: Them)
gonna do? What can They do but pretend to be "specialists"
called in to save the poor bastard from the Grinning
Reaper's ice-caress "just in the nick of Time" (Time doesn't
nick: it bites: hard) so he can accrue more debt?

Dead Men have no coverage. Eligibility is rendered null-
void the instant meat divorces mind.

Whatever. Find someone to lay with and be etherized.
Smoke a doob if it'll calm you down.

Good-luck. Au river. Ciao. See ya.

Humanisms

Spine of My Time

Declared "adult" at eighteen — though still a resident of Father's home — I matured admirably.

Across the river spread the shore of my nineteenth year: aroused and glistening. Summer of sun sand song. Girls young to love — not as daughters: lovers: then — and wine and sway and moving Toward: looking Toward. Confident-impatient. Forward toward Forward-Toward: never look back.

At forty I turned twenty-one and they were dead: all of them: the ones I'd struggled to impress.

Deceased. Address unknown. Gone.

The Old Man too. Da. Da. Gone.

What wrenched the spine of my Time crooked: maimed the Smithy of my Soul: stopped growth and movement — once feral-audacious — at the brink?

What sneeze of fate flash-froze me at the onset of Emerge?

The Then then: and then: slow hammering to upright. Painful worked the crippled Smithy. Facing grief: loss: mortality: with mannish eyes.

I'd like to call it Wisdom rather than defeat: but really I would rather swim — back: to the forward of my shore.

Punctuation Space

First things first is figure out who you were. Punctuation space: hiatus of character — still: yet: again. The cracked Eternal over-easy. Infinite Ever-After.

Vape of e-lectronic cigarette the clock-watcher's impatient suck: killing (at least wounding? hardly a scratch really) Time.

Before page-glut deletion-crunch per data-measures of Determine: before everything useless crumpled tossed.

beyond place

It's nice beyond the dreams of lies of platitudes of Future speeding drunk head-on (I haven't a thing to wear): must we see more — again?

Does anyone remember used-to-be of Know?

I recall fear-of. Fear-of being: fear-of fearing: fear-of fear as being:

like:

the naked free in strange wood: dead: fat legs exposed.

It's nice beyond the terrible beyond-place. I wish you were here. I wish I were not you.

Eminence

"It was better before before they voted for" (Exene Cervenka
and John Doe, X)

So much pain for so many except the ones already wiped out
bought out sold out to the dummy-down: down:

down.

Don't wanna be no smarty-pants or nuthin' like that.

"Like whaddya think yer better'n everbody else?"

"Maybe. What if I do? My thoughts my mind. I can imagine
my Self better than anyone I know."

How did it all start? The End I mean. Was it like this "in the
beginning?" One of those Zen Koan Twilight Zone paradox
trips?

Surely Rod Serling grinning smoke will tell us:

"It's always been like this. At least since vaudeville. Relax.
Loosen your ties bras girdles: eat beef: drink Manhattans. Play
cards: bowl. Enjoy The Empire while it's still in black-and-
white..."

stop shy of extreme

Lateralize scope-focus of applied cruelty from confessional to onomatopoeic.

Note: stop shy of extreme.

Empire cannibalizing Empire: nineteen-seventy-something Woody Allen angst about "the universe expanding."

Tedious.

The problem with neurotic solipsists is no proportion-process relative to when the sky heave-staggers: phlegm of rain an omen-ominous: slouched exhaustion-shoulders hint collapse.

Possibly: but at its own pace — slow: not our acceleration-gasps of Red Alert.

Honestly.

Nothing's funny anymore: *nein* zip *nein* zing. They've cut the balls off humor: among other things. Always "time enough to rot" after the ravings of a *kvetch.*

The spark-cackles of true hysteria are meaty and defiant: arch. They compel us to imagine Climate: they plot changes radical-profound: puzzling homage to suns that never shine — however unctuous and abject kneel the faithful.

True religion offers risk not guarantee. No drips: nor virgins sacrificed to flat-screen alters in high definition

if
 supported:
else:
     consult manual:
     message Help Desk:
     contact manufacturer:
or
 scream

```
        for details
end if
```

Lexicon

Cease and desist your cosmic-karmic baby-talk: your inspirational chit-chat banter: your learnéd shuck'n'jive — immediately: if not sooner.

Trash smash pulverize or burn all fashionably ridiculous notions whispered earnestly in dark rooms among the hip morbid narcissistic baffled but of course deeply concerned.

Spineless soul-less spiritual laws of Positive Attraction: Critique of Pure Sports Ritual: Metaphysic of Mumbo-Jumbo: a broken harmonica and a bent kazoo.

Good? Evil? Surely we're Beyond Wood and Anvil at this point: no?

Suppose we agreed: all "stranger things in heaven and on earth Horatio" are-were-ever-been mere patterns of semiotic such such such: linguistic over-run of system-flow.

'Nuff said.

Signifier sign-symbols goose-step cell to synapse: spark of thought-emotion human-all-too-human and such-like razzmatazz: exchange of sight-sound among meatish minds perish soon forgotten.

But if written recorded disbursed gather momentum: reach critical mass: merge-with-overtake Reality.

Just chat after all: extended and replayed: begun as kitchen-talk comparisons of recipes culled from grandmother's precision steel box of index-card noesis.

"Pinch of morpheme: dash of phoneme: twist two turns style-syntax. Salt and spice to taste."

Repeated accepted retained: print-recorded on-line-off: under aegis of Lexicon: with full Authority over the powers invested therein.

War Lost in the Database

lemme go dear lemme go dear lemme go
to the
war lost in the database: bedlam bedlam obfuscation:
imagine such perplex of half a million soldiers: vehicles:
personnel to distant shores:
track all units: error-margin slim: planes bomb non-existent
cities: targets that did not exist before the raids emerged to
be flattened: risen laid low:
so many planes recalled mid-mission: obliteration scream
of blood-confusion: cities mistaken alive unscheduled
unplanned: paperwork: investigation: disarray...
NEVERTHELESS...
... if holidays surveyed by cops in hats will not relax you
nothing will. In circuitry we're wireless amazed together
in the sweet by-and-by: the hole between us — wide as a
whale's cervix — is expanding...

Rutting Stars

We are human all too human hungry wolves run wild over hills: through streams and forests: life-times.

Sweat-blood-sex-shriek: Night's ecstatic feed.

Alone together we raise demigods and smoke.

Afterward: "Thank you. Night."

Salt-metal exchange lingers nostalgic on our tongues.

Rutting stars — unseen — pierce moonbeams dawn to dusk.

Memo from Headquarters:

Penetrate: excavate: drill deep the meat-bone.

Shell confession: her description — absent analysis — meaningless as "Sorry."

Punishment is process. Penalties accrue. Climaxes apply — sequentially addressed.

Impetus of inquiry: defendants rendered grim beyond control. Primitive spin of vinyl grooves in analog. Translated: obviated: superannuated: inside-outside up-down-forwarded unto asynchronous exile (eventually indexed "lost" — absolutely-irrecoverably — to the Database of Power).

Deliberate prisoners manacled to clock-ticks monitor expensive day-nights of Confused. Unwanted. Irrelevant-useless: just shy of perverse.

"This must not be" think prisoners at labor (and in). "Even if I must not be to make damned sure this is not was not no way in hell ever will be. Never-ever…"

Quantum Creep

Punched by photons before breakfast: clocked cold. He'd never seen so many stars break day: nor ever had one socked him.

Another same-old-same-old sleepless night in space-time-continuous as always ever is-was-been: however: when dawn's rose-fingered digits beamed a clock-time reasonable to rise he rose — reasonably — to switch the switch.

That was when Light smacked hard: that was when Life became uncertain.

Later in the pool he swam with sperm the size of Tiger Sharks: squishy-gross like water-balloons: gray eyeless determined.

They attacked: they attacked: they attacked till — slackened — stopped: wasted by chlorine (he kept a tidy pool).

Dead sperm floated belly-up. Like tadpoles. What had they sought from him?

Were they hostile particles? Or blinded mad by unknown passions unappeased: nascent zealots swimming salmon-like in egg-ward waves — snatched en route to bliss — as shocked as he was by their sudden Here? And just as certainly uncertain?

He feared what possibilities might drop next through hidden chutes of hours remaining to this weird irregular and spooky same old same-old day.

rummaging

A step away from naked: dream-shocked: mortal: shivering ghosts of young. Firm stabbing routine: decay not profit: bah-sheep bah-sheep shorn again: fleeced numb.

Forever-days merge everywhere-time: dates swell — throbbing worse-to-come. That sudden leap from Then to Now: impending burn of bulk-life: supplies of want-some far exceed demand for ever-more. Plummeting shares a head-ache no one needs. Notorious motions-toward augur extremes.

Skeptical experts regard the bottom-out — skeptically.

"Panic of bump-snag" They say.

"The come-down-down still decades hence" They say.

"Hysterics stubbed the Monster's cloven toe: however: the beast ain't dead — yet" They say.

"Yes yes yes: formal obsequies make famous: stiff-but-subtle journalese obits mark two-bit know-names known-forgotten: necrologies dish dirt: black-hole guesstures collapse bottomless-empty the plaster minds of statue-folk. However: sparks don't kindle forest fires: read between the lies" They say.

"Possibility demands regardless: stark relief against particular: amateur conjecture damns the consequence. The future of eat or if demands vim-vigor see to binding see" They say — to the cadaver: bound trussed cuffed.

Impotent rage at stone reflections: mirrors you'll return to hit some one responsible for all this lacking: an essential not-forgotten. Like a dance done well: few notice it's there and fewer once it's gone.

energy needs

Salmon are dying: eaten by bears who need jobs: insurance: hibernation-leave — with pay.

"This clean energy source does not pollute the air!"

Plenty to come. Starts on the dot. Size of a period. Final emphatic:

egg.

"Hurry darling you're way past fifteen minutes."

Crushed-lost in people-thickets teem-frothing expert shoppers. Notorious consumers oiled and supple once bathed drugged under Flamenco sun: tanned delicate as flan — a prescription for sleep with government warning: sleeplessness memory-loss death may occur: consult a physician or someone responsible or someone who cares that salmon perish for rage of bears: disenfranchised-unemployed: anxiety-depressed: starved. No bread no Health no Pharma: no cave of one's own.

Fruit of Occur

Despair distilled of sad. Wine of Know turned vinegar Now.

Fruit of occur: no scent no bloom: origin empty.

Matter — stark mad dark — metastasized: full-bloat increase unto pregnant Void.

Those who invent History tend to delete it. Eradicate you with a mouse-click keystroke dead-link subject to oversight by Editors who hate you.

There was a Time: it's gone.

But On Sale Today through Next Time: pain-kill pills and terror: theft of Identity construct (bureaucro-systemic amnesia).

They'll slash yer credit to yer toe-nails — postmortems rarely pay-up. They'll render you post facto: DNA unclaimed: your name null-void: a number irrational beyond equation: illegible to machines.

So here's your Now now: enjoy: don't blow a bender play it safe: choose door one-two: sell lady mortgage tiger. Time is money-season: ticktock-tick a bomb.

Burn in infer.

Squinting Reach to Touch

Squinting reach to touch — a childhood scene.

Years ago an awe-struck girl: a teen-ager: my first fixation from afar: my first anonymous: my first air-suck of "Wow."

I bathed in her emission.

Perhaps she's someone's mother or grandmother or alone or sharing life-accumulated with some strange man or woman far-away-from and indifferent-to my Me: my existence in her reduced to moments years ago she caught me watching: otherwise — for all she knew: to the extent she could recall: deep as memory can plunge — I do not live: I did not live: nor had I ever could-have-would-have lived.

Perhaps she is someone somewhere: watching.

Everyone Always: Watching

They're out there watching. Beyond stuffiness: beyond conformity: beyond the nest.

Eyes all the time now: eyes all the time now: static: watching. Ghosts.

So many images of you and me: peas' crucible: cosmic porridge: the soup-vanishing: poof.

Me and you since the beginning of the den: poised posed relaxed: lifetimes prepared for cameras watching: audience: everyone always watching: nothing to it.

The Expert we watched said it "was difficult to conduct: the model was difficult: to demonstrate on-screen."

He had intended to show us how to laugh: but the smart-gadget he'd built from wire old wood and spare parts imploded: collapsed-endless in upon itself soon as the Expert man — with not a little flourish — turned the knob: to demonstrate: to "show them how it's done..."

Cursive Fortune Cookie

Before ideas went bad: before ridiculous notions of generals in hats: my Shadow fled the mirror: zip-zap-gone: god-knows-where...

I'd made an impression: or dream-imagined memories of Me vague-brief as sleep.

Woke up devastated and alarmed: the 20 years that passed through Night were Yesterday ten years ago. Had been. Was.

Failing to cultivate Selective Consciousness I remain mired in situations on the ground.

Hat Club

For the last time I implore you:
please restrict your hat:
forbid it entry to the hat-club.

Correct me if I'm wrong again
but: say you're sorry.
And for god-sake mean it:
all will be forgiven.

I love you dearly
darling
tell me what you're thinking.
Darling:
tell me what you feel.

Trigger Moments

Left-jab every tick right-cross each tock. Relentless fusillade: rocks hurled hard — deliberate — by meaner stronger faster clocks than I have known. Until Tomorrow shows its muscle should Tomorrow come — for me.

Look back on moments not years. They're yours the moments. Always were. Not even Time-addiction to Decline can shuck-and-junk your times in Time or sway your mind to focus on attacks to come: more painful than Yesterday's yet tolerable: relative to savageries relentless masked Tomorrow guarantees to shock not please.

"I am The Day:" boasts Tomorrow: clock-work-cruel young-vigorous: hinting ambush — always — within chaos-traffic of Today.

Perhaps — even now — Tomorrow squats patiently: disguised as Moment: triggered to explode.

Imagine Aliens: an Introduction

Imagine aliens observing work of days:

What specimens these humans be! Wonders to behold. Such heights so few attain. The rest are ink-blots: scenery: mass-gelatinous: *der Volk*.

Observe them typing memos: business-letters: urgent poems.

Study the path-process of sequence.

How gracefully they dream-sluice gales of Time!

Recognition happens slow: descending like an egg.

"They see what they want to see:" ain't no cliché: they notice when they need to notice what they need to not-ignore.

Assume the words to conjure fields crossed in 'the day.' When you were tuned-in-aware. Not like now: you're so damned good-cop-bad-cop tense-confused: must be thousands like you: millions: prognosticators of doom-gloom and bad-hair days.

How are their works and days? More importantly: why?

They know what they are: "killer brilliant mind-blowing" slaves — of desire.

Unfulfilled.

Bare Legs on Camera

Summer between states out in the country: code-red intimacies: fights none could avoid. Word-shock assault of scimitar-wit: thrust-parry-thrust-dodge. Judo utterance. Weapons of mass irony and cake.

The Vanquished waved white handkerchiefs of wry surrender: touché.

We laughed: we had fun.

Someone said "nonplussed" out on the porch. "Nonplussed" we chanted in clumsy chorus at bungalows and trees. Again and again and again: we sang it like a song.

Cameras caught sudden-risibles — snap-flash — candidly obscene: hysteric whoop-raucous of instant. So many instants cherished at the time: mute photographs' flat recall. Now fading in the attic. Cramming boxes in the basement.

Holographic memories of you beside me on camera: bare legs exposed: on camera: you beside me bare legs exposed: on camera.

Our hazy forest-leafy green and rainy-always season in the hills. City-mice among the gnarled gruff weather-beaten taciturn and morbid folk. No fun.

But we were fun.

We had Future and our own familiar forms: The Guys: the Girls. So termed in even longer-ago-days of teen-age composite. Eternal crowd of Always: our crowd: always: admired from afar: envied by ones who wanted to be or at least be like us: whoever we were: or thought we were back-when.

Plus other ego-psych stuff odd and sundry: I kept records.

Meanwhile at the Country Fair:

Makers of lutes tabors mandolins and other country-folk

wood banjo-things hawked boxes of dulcimer carved from pine.

"Wonderfully shaped and smooth of sound" they told us. Sinuous. Easy to learn.

"You'll soon be strumming away the sultry-lazy Summer days. Strumming in yon noble wood on lyres of yon noble wood composed" they said.

We bought three lutes: one mandolin. The woman tossed in a tabor: gratis.

I remember a thin girl at Ye Olde-Tyme Country Donut Booth. She hesitated over a cruller — waist on her mind: what you said to me after: you said:

"Makes me feel old"

really we were still so very young the week-end of the Fair: I couldn't understand because we really all were still so very young...

Later the same Fair another booth like the lute-box woman's but with flutes and fifes. Four hand-carved recorders completed our blow-string-drum ensemble: old-time flute-things expert-crafted by real folk. Objects of beauty: value: practical use. Genuine stuff. Surely Classics by now: antiques.

What was that shindig I made sure to miss two years ago? Twenty-year reunion? The tense-passing of two years felt like thirty...

I stashed the lute somewhere I can't recall. Never learned to play: but that wasn't the point the point was Experience. Life-mind memories of life well-lived. Should you lose memory or marbles you've got pictures: in whatever basement boxes they remain wherever sealed.

Yes. Yes. Yes. Soon. Yes: call me. Yeah: dinner: just us: it'll be just us.

Time is the New Black (London: March 2000)

Time is the new black. In London it was gray.

March umbrella season we carried and concealed. Nothing immoral or illegal: I don't think. Indifference: jet-lag: ennui.

Morning mother-lode: drugged sleep pushed hard: a heavy chest upon my heaving chest.

"Do not get up: do not walk aimless through this foreign city: do not move."

Re-dosed: pressed on: it was vacation.

The Victoria and Albert museum: established in a gush of Royal concern for the education: instruction: and amusement of loyal subject peasant heirs to Empire's perpetual sunset and the colors it revealed.

Victoria and Al (and family) magnanimously bequeathed unto *der Volk* entire attics clutter-crammed with Albion's old junk. Mostly hot: local loot lifted from yokel land-lubbers: but also: vast properties Her Majesty's Navy "discovered" abroad and conquered colonized or wasted out-right: *sans* trinkets *sans* treaty. "No tickee no shirtee: Bub."

A passel of statues: Buddhas and Saints: Knights on catafalques: centuries of Fashion redacted and revised. Old scalps skins spears rugs: foundation art-myth-dream-relics: legacies. Every tribe its totems and taboos: its language and its legends — imperial life force thrust like bayonets through broken cultures. Languages dead-gutted: rotting unrecorded.

A: kill grammar B: siphon lexicon

English knack of grafting words of conquered peoples' colorful slang and idiom to status of Official-Usage per Language of Empire and Conquest. Preterit grammar long ago discarded: shucked shell of intimacies past: gibberish.

Time is the new black: you'll wear it everywhere: believe me.

Percocet amphetamine espresso forward: an acceleration:

The Future was Now: we took advantage. We drank "bitter:" took promenades and cigarettes in Hyde Park. Sunny seventy degrees and not yet Spring. Cost a pound to piss at Harrod's. Then uniformed attendants shook me down for more. Total thrift shop damage of your kerchief plus my blazer half the price of a piss in Harrod's posh latrine — fully-serviced and peer-reviewed — not including tip.

This was real London stuff real England.

Eggs sausage and blood-pudding: workmen wolfing fat to burn through drudgery of Hours: the process can take years.

Street-beggars — most un-Dickensian — held sacks of kids not gin: babes they'd birthed or sired — one assumed — while refugees or something poor-ish and Romantic.

Not like boozers whom it's fun to snub. Yeah I'm a boozer: but I wouldn't have given me a dime in The Day nor accepted one from a bum such as myself.

Outside of Life and Time: moments words once carried don't compute concretely can't compete with image-objects time-stamped data-based mis-reproduced.

I'm bored I'm restless I'm uncertain: irrelevant: possibly done: I don't know I'm not sure.

"Tomorrow we'll avoid the eggs."

Purgatory

Too many people pack heat eat meat don't recycle languish costly-long in showers: gimme-gimme-age of me-first decadence: we're doomed.

Don't worry about me I'll be fine.

Really it's OK to watch it all collapse and burn: brings closure: emotional growth: pride: acceptance: whatever vice-virtue's virally in vogue. Self-Esteem.

I hope to kill myself before I die: I hate surprises.

Lost interest in my own narrative: shit happens — or doesn't: didn't. Grew bored of predictable: of random-absurd. Forget yer plot-twists I want soliloquy: oratory: a microphone: a soap-box: glottal genesis: inspiration of my Me: *sui generis*.

Could I have been a better person? Would anyone have cared? I gave much: loved hard not long. I never harmed a one — without just cause: nor did I lie much cheat or steal.

If there's any way out please let me know. Truly I'm stumped. Do send your thoughts.

Prayers too why not: but only if you must.

Blunder Gaze of Cosmic Eye

1.

From Decay

Botched job in the kitchen. The wretched boy refused Death's protocol progression from decay to rot to never-been: and similar trends from which The Strong derive.

2.

None Fulfilled

Ten million stories none fulfilled.

If Past won't change what is: what is to come? And when?

Patterns of action-movement brought no Be: not much doing: nothing done.

Facsimiles of movement forged by repetition. Much said nothing done.

3.

Plotting Sorts-of-Sit

Plotting sorts-of-sit: derivatives of sat.

Attempts to replicate the rush of musk allure: as-if entranced by potent tinctures of herself.

As-if: yesterday's high.

Enough as-if to lure as Lure itself had lured — long time ago. As-if effused her being and her telling: vernacular of consequence: speech-tick: My-Tale signal: evidence of Self.

Evidence not proof: but still: inspired strong imperatives of

Love that Love delighted in repeating.

Each one must explain what makes one one: eventually.

Not yet.

For anyone could understand if anyone would know: that what had been should have been without regret as consequence of might have could have would have been.

Second-guess of deep-absurd: ridiculous in pull-back relative to all that's been and all who've suffered — and to what extent — the blunder gaze of Cosmic Eye.

But still: the second guess: the third...

4.

Pain and Loss

Dead kid in a slip-shod kitchen.

Love's wretched life-course (murder of Self? abort of Other?). Pain and Loss.

Desire for completion or extreme. These are difficult themes. Love attempted to transform. Smoke of heartless drift a bitter blow: oh: Empty Memory of shadow-strangers in the glass!

5.

Protagonist Love Interest

I knew Love. A difficult complete. Consistently. One two three slips here-there mere error: perhaps odd — perverse? — penchant for novelty: tilting *avant garde*.

But:

consistency is pattern: pattern is pathology.

Love had problems. I loved Love. I had problems.

Pattern.

6.

Night Entered with Drama

I tried to talk then fuck Love to completion.

Pain ensued and Loss.

Long ago we saw trees bloom sooty flowers in the park and we resolved to solve what-ever resolve — and teaching fellowships — would solve for once and god-damned all.

First time this life I knew core definition of hard-deep: but could not leave the only world I'd ever known.

Night entered with drama: velvet cape of terrifying atmosphere. Confusion-frightened of Time's brevity I dreaded physical decline.

7.

Recollections of What's Never Been

The Kid believed in Dad.

Wherefore why-for whence this vanishing of Home?

Filmic mind-stuff: recollections of what's-never-been: spectral street-banquets of everything-everywhere-and-all sucked life-blood from what lived: as-if not born of Love: as-if Love splashed smoldering glands with cold white paint: a cagey ruse to dodge pain-tedium completely heinous to conceive: token of lunatic dreams sown long-faraway ago.

8.

Mute Gesture Command

Proximity of Home disturbed me to disgust with full intent to mock: possessed of a hate too intimate-revealing of one's first-expose — in awe-repulse — to mute gesture command: of life: of consequence. My virgin score.

9.

Furious Camouflage

I daydreamed more than mere possession: proprioception: saw furious camouflage in membranes of Love's womb.

So many moments etched on skin distorted to weird and worse by Time: grim patriarch: progenitor of Pain and Loss.

10.

Ghosts Laughed at My Suit

Alone in Love's botched kitchen I was exhausted.

Ghosts laughed at my suit: poor tired spirits: demented by Night's forced after-death parade through desert-smears of Pain and Loss: to each his own significance and Other.

Experience amplified thunderous: repeated and exchanged: like prisoners trade cigarettes: dream-currency of trapped-entombed.

11.

Completion

Confusion staggered after Night alone. Resolution pounded feral at the door. Desire smashed my daze of words with palpable thingness of a weapon.

Steel-bone recognition: not-Pain not-Loss not-Love nor any other.

I cocked aimed fired my last first sentence to completion.

Blood of Night

Exit 40: Map to From

Wherever they were was not quite there. They spoke in earnest: Blood and Night: to themselves and to each other.

Their proximity of birth — in separate hospitals: within hours of receiving names — was gravid with meaning: applauding each his/her forever-license to live comic to the core: high on laughter: high on love: pursuit of Being to the Nth degree: alone together.

They owned their lives: hence mutual indifference to regard — of others.

Blood and Night: sought-after undesirables: risible: insouciant: young. Open to antics of the confident wry-earnest (even when faced with soul-crushing defeat): open to all who claimed the planet Home. Anything that satisfied: anything on earth to give: graciously: and gracious to receive.

Those who live such fantasies as Blood and Night believe themselves destined to liberate in-yer-face but arcane symbols Commentary seals: a series of next-lines branched like fractals from comic extensions of discourse: moments brought sacred stuff of text breathing applause.

The Audience: owners of focus: for whose amusement: enlightenment: awe: such beings as Blood and Night perpetually played humble fake-it-till-you-make-it quest of value: significance: Home.

Applause like incense to those who lived Life live: before the omnipresent Unseen: before cameras committed all to scrutiny: celebrity: the screech-laughter of fools. They would roll as far as possible on earth to roll: and give what was desired always-evermore by all: once they figured out precisely what was sought (thin margin of error a diaphanous sheath) what deep-core satisfaction bought approval even in stillest stillness of attainable hours watched passionately in secret by The Unseen — whether or not one was a Celebrity to be celebrated on camera or a Nobody nothing insect — another re-spite: to be scrutinized: analyzed: surveyed.

Blood — wry in his black suit: anxiety wound tight around a common gut-core of despair: and Night — droll erotic spider: fearless black frock black pumps. Together they studied maps of Toward and From: where Make began: where-ever Where-Ever might be. Surely a guide lived who might lead them.

"Maybe not of Space but Time. Is there a map of Time?" asked Night.

"We really gotta get back" said Blood. "Become inspired — if possible — again. Or at least get off this wretched go-Me trip. My mind's blown senseless."

"We're not too bad. Relative to others I've seen" she said.

"Who: the scribblers?" asked Blood.

"Scribblers: recorders: photo-geneticists: typists — keepers of Preserve. The people of Perpetuation — and caffeine."

"Their Selves extended like hands to shake" he said.

"Yes. Them. The ones who infuse all interactions — from text-talk to face-to-face Real Time — with not-selves: as each try to convince the other as well as themselves that radical minutes had been lived. Or better: that all the blasted years had been fantastic seasons of a dream: that somewhere something deep (it's always 'deep:' gotta be: sure ain't apparent on the surface) within themselves had-been/still-was of certain value and would endure — for at least a few years — in someone's diary: address book: enemies list: something — anything — that might be found and seen — if only as a dead-site or social-net obituary on the Network" quoth Night.

She screwed a new tip onto her customized e-lectronic cigarette: offered a fresh disposable to him.

"Yeah" said Blood exhaling genuine-tobacco-flavored steam. "I can pretend my Self is just a matter of struggling toward some distant Some-day: that this black-hole pursuit of infinities: abstractions: symbols dense with — what else? — yet further equal-but-opposite pursuits: as in opposite direction: as in: 'you've been on the wrong path from the get-go buddy:' that all this 'I must know how much knowing I must know' will make sense in a not-too-distant confluence of cosmic wombs and all things sacred and eternal and all that. But I don't know. I'm weary — and wary — of folks with Big Ideas: Grand Theories: Ridiculous Notions."

"Let's get drunk" Night said.

Too drunk to stagger home: a car arrived to take them. Forty-five minutes from The City. Miles and miles it must have been: the driver drove hard. Chrystal Night looked to the camera-man who wasn't there then to the comic man who was: beside her in the back-seat of the limo: semi-conscious: slightly less coherent than herself.

"Drive" she said to the man behind the wheel: "We have to finish."

"Excuse me?" the driver asked.

"Alone together: far away" she slurred.

"Another day begins at mid-night" the driver said. "In terms of fare. Plus service charge and tax the total."

"Drive" she said. Turning to Blood: "Where we going?"

"Home. Exit 40" eyes shut.

"Exit 40!" Night said to the driver.

"Yes ma'am."

"Got it right: roughly?"

What on earth to give?

"Exit 40" the driver repeated.

Map to From. It almost feels: thought she.

The Pit

The first word Blood invented and the debut of a second: ages ago when they were kids.

The area's connected now: split-levels spread wide-far: but there's the old school football field and track — weatherbeaten stands not weatherbeaten but fresh-kept-well — electric scoreboards on both sides. Gone were the trees lots fields of the eight-to-eighteen-age years both Blood and Night recalled.

They were seventeen the night Blood spoke to Night atop the Pit then in the Pit not far in the woods but far enough: dug-deep. Sharing coffee and glazed donuts he told her of The Pit's epic construction by Blood and compeers: fourteen-year-olds — impressive impressionable — at the time.

Blood said:

"We built a Pit — odd name for kids to — oh yeah: Joseph: his brothers ripped off his colors (a gang or tribe thing I suppose) and tossed him in a Pit: sold him to slave-traders. Not this Pit: we were fourteen: ripe for a club-house underground: in the woodsy unfinished (i.e. wild) section of the park frequented by no one except cops and freaks at night: 'Spider Park' — swings sand-box kids and monkey-bar things shaped like spiders hence its unofficial name.

"We planned The Pit on paper: gathered materials early spring at night (scraps discarded by construction crews erecting malls McMansions office parks). We dug the impression — six feet wide: six feet long: six feet deep: lay down floor-boards and erected walls. We measured cut hammered sawed and futzed in strict accordance with design. We worked after school and week-ends after little-league base-ball. We finished by June.

"The Girls brought weed and beer to celebrate. There were the Guys and the Girls. The Guys played sports and built the Pit: a place to make out with the Girls. We all went Dutch on booze and weed. Fun-times to recall: Sex Drugs Rock

N' Roll Spring nights probing genitals and music: cramp-crowded like a van carpeted wall to-wall: the street-sign we stole clean-polished and hung on a nail read: Yield."

clear nights under stars of home-grown beautiful:
down in The Pit The-Guys The-Girls: energy hit
hard who fondled to caress deeper the source-core
ecstatic Greater-Than in deepest Us: profound:

"The Pit flooded warped molded after the first hard rain. We caulked the trap-door entrance with putty: didn't work completely: but complete enough.

"The cops sent to shut us down approached all Big-Man beefy: saw workmanship and guts: we were fourteen: their blue minds blown: we were kids. They pounded the walls open-closed the trap-door pretended to inspect: pretended to be satisfied: pretended it was safe: this thing they wished they could have built themselves back in The Day: before dark uniforms and head-cracking blood-sweat-blues: before rude jokes and beers. 'Be careful' they cautioned or 'Be good' or some such crap. Then they were gone. Did they know what they'd witnessed — those cops — how unique-special and profound? Kids create and kids destroy according to their options: but a project like this. Worthy of Pharaoh."

"So Pharaoh: what's next? " asked Night.

Night Blood: a Romance

Latin *part partit:*

many social factions divide to share come-together-sex music
and loud laughter: distressing:

if:

　"that is it"

then:

　"must it be?"

and:

　"why?"

end if

Aristophanes: Symposium: shared parts: whole depart one-again
not fade away to day-break-dawn: and like-minded pleasures.

Strictly business:

darkish wettish
Lava Ho's
gathering-gathering
is *bad* for business:
specifically: ours.
Get *ridda da Ho:*
by any mean necessity.

Overhead television red-eye-stoned: points entered:
departures revoked.

Chorus of 1000 gay rabbis (Hasidim: I think) chants: "you
you you."

Indeed television: joke ubiquitous: Entertainent-News blather. Re-runs of Might Possibly Be So.

Blood and Night ate donuts — glazed: gazed nowhere at nothing: remembered community: scenic environs of youth upstream: conscious of attention: span the final show: to be Big Fish.

High violence of comedy: a bloodless coup: hypnotic humor: folks piss their pants: their heads explode. That's entertainment. Killer sell-point: comedy is killer.

"He kills me!"

Daddy-O said: "Top of the charts: number-one-smash or die. Hey: I'm not kidding."

Chorus of The Confused chants: "you you you."

./ said:

Subjective Communication and Relational Arts Meta-language and Build Operator: or SCRAMBO. The system itself: the operating system. The "OS."

./ said:

Subjective Communication and Relational Arts Meta-language. SCRAM. That is: the language of the system per se. Scrambonics: Semiotics of Scram (SOS) — compression and division of Deep Scram to manageable threads via short-hand script. Hence: Language of Scrambonic Transfer (LOST).

./ (bored-impatient) said:

Scram-based Operating System. SOS. Base Operations System Scram. BOSS. Scram-up: Scram from scratch. All rights ruthlessly reserved.

./'s Crack-byte team concluded kernel trans-code meta-SCRAM core Scrambo update process of virtual load integration:

or:

"Software can be..."

Weird like naked and the bedroom door behind them.

Night: "Look how weirded-out they — "

Blood: "Just watching"

Night: "Real to them"

Blood: "Real as TV"

Night: "Weird like naked: us watching us"

Blood: "Blood and Night made flesh — salaciously conspicuous"

Night: "Real to those kids"

Blood: "Screen all their lives"

Night: "House their house"

Blood: "Once mine"

Explosive limitless Language of Technology (LanTech): words are numbers: you know: like Kaballah: so they say: I've never read it.

Anyway: not funny a guy can't humor his own speech: so I learned Naked: fluently: pronounced with sonorous diction.

Transcripts titled DUBBED: a voice (whose?) allegedly

knows whether B = C circuit data-mined meta-characters of SCRAMBO.

Language of Scrambonic Transfer (LOST): Practical Eye Extension Protocol (PEEP): Semiotics of Scram (SOS).

Configuration instant: compiled immediate: on-the-fly: Real Time. Matter density of line per substance layer of bandwidth times speed-of-light (almost) to the Nth power of ten: or eight: doesn't matter really: just rough-guesstimating tomes of girlish glyphs round anorexic: one zero zero one zero zero:

one.

Machines hold product of withdrawn: largest cigar detonated: ever: boom: ten-kiloton blast! Technology: virtually limitless what we can do.

Data expertise of language code is 90 percent mental the other half drugs: binary string one zero one zero: zero zero: one:

OR

IF/ELSE

NOT WHILE

THEN DO

Alpha Function()

Beta Function()

of our

YES/NO

AND/OR

IF/ELSE

THEN:

code-expression object-origin = alpha-numeric of our IF and OR.

Application code example Free Taste core of kernel: score a sample: Free taste Free! Toll Free!

Blood: "SCRAMB-O SCRAM-BO SCRAAAAA-AAAAM-BOOOOOOOOH"

One needs human precious forward or the next adventure rules. Regard: observers lurk subjective:

Blood: "Gee whiz that's an awful lotta"

Night: "Maniacs"

Blood: "But smart"

Night: "Frightening"

Blood: "There's that"

Night: "Less ain't more"

Blood: "Language of"

Night: "Machines"

Blood: "The Future"

Night: "None that I can see"

Regarding growth-expansion: Real needs seeds: however: exceptions develop: conceptual disputes regarding tree-structure hierarchies:

"Just whaddya mean by 'Superuser?'"

The real question: which sub-lingo of LOST might fuel stars: ignite dark matter: bloom networks infinite: if only in theory: metaphor: dream?

./:

Universe to build whatever on and on.

Night:

Infinite relational: and rational.

Blood:

Sc-sc-sc-scrambo.

./:

Gonna fuck'em all — and how. Big time. Despite dubious...

Night:

Every last whisper: dignity of Self.

./:

Anything mine ain't theirs.

Blood:

Fundamental wrong. On some level: I think. Why only yesterday...

./:

Botched opportunities. Spilled milk. Over-inflated value of their own lost time: and stupefaction. Sick cows flooded the market with bad karma. Moo. Moo. Beginning of the end.

Send the sick cows home. Better yet: fuck'em! Fuck 'em all.

Blood:

It literally at least hypothetically can be —

./:

Such tiny slivers of human-be: like bugs.

Night:

So?

./:

Evolve!

Blood:

Again?

./:

Get on with it! By any mean necessity.

Blood:

"The plains below are empty of Indians" the cow-boy-hatted commentator said on TV. He was talking about a canvas displayed in The Fact Museum as part of the new Frontier Art craze with tie-ins about the cultural/historical importance of MoneyFast Destiny. "The victims of MoneyFast Destiny never ceased to haunt American art" crooned TV Cowboy. "Where are your lands now?" hissed TV Cowboy's Boss.

Crazy Horse replied: "My lands are where my dead lie buried."

To which Boss snidely remarked: "Well fuck you Crazy Man: we just bought up all that land and now we got the legal right throw your red ass the hell off it!"

So Crazy-Horse killed him: but not without much sorrow —

not much sorrow at all really: none.

./:

So? What's your point?

Hey Daddy-0:
those were the days
of fast pink cars:
long-sleek aqua fins:
martinis dry real dry:
stretch-limousine days
of more make-more
characters none craved:
so they endured.

The Infocracy's aesthetic prime directive regarding music
and the so-called Arts remains consistent: hell you are hell
you are hell you are hell you are hell you are hell you are.

Program music 10101010101010101:

[[Object = SELF
{like you mean
{don't speak of
{conformity
+ stuffiness
== nest}
they're out there:
watching:
too many eyes all the
time now:
too much:
if
not Life
then
print: "My electric ghost"}

```
}}
]
(ghost = SELF NEW)
]
```

So many tragedies of photograph: analog: digital: flat: 3D.
Stilled moments of my Me. Eyes of the world unite peas
porridge hot: cramped crucible.   Anyway Night might
vanish: poof.

You and me since my Me first determined to attempt to try
to become himself. Didn't care who he actually was: or what
kind of Self he would become. Beyond good and evil and all
that. But really: since the beginning...

Lifetime preparation: raised on camera watched-watching:
poised posed relaxed: always: nothing to it: each kid issued
clean plastic relation to age-mates: instilled-impressed in
unison together: en mass.

Photos of Blood: Night beside him bare legs on camera. Grade
people on wondering. Tears of those who never displayed.

Creation of performance character: what people seem.
Further along in the text: Blood of is always was will be. His
comic Me: his moment-instant — fictional: of course.

Pause sentence music for Brand-awareness of narrative-
action-character.

Scene:

"Perhaps her own good: can't always 'just move on.'"

Another moment-instant: fictional.

Wondering Chrystal's tears who never displayed what people seem. Further along in the text: Blood of was always is: his will-creation as performance-character: his cosmic comic Blood: moment-instant of "Can't always 'just move on.'"

The strange we called home: alien beds mistaken for long-ago's that never were. His own under-the-covers warm again think talk again: house been house been his house: his transpire: where Time happened.

One upon the other bring the restless kid-pile party close. Gather ritual youth together. The kind of anywhere-time "Welcome!" young folks like. Time and place for house their own divided had lived away far-leaving: multiply-accrue: invite alone-together time-place to convene: orders of magnitude: request delivery no questions asked.

Many social factions divide to share come-together sex-music: if that is it then must it be and why?

Inn Sanity: down-city-abandoned almost-homes of blasted hives. Callista Noh: hostess.

Café Insanity: bar: rooms: Network-Movies-Television.

Meanwhile upstairs...

Callista's husband ./ and staff ran the Crack-byte Net-site and SCRAMBO development-testing lab. Fronting (infiltrating?) the Third LAN?

Blood: "Room at The Inn?"

Callista: "Sanity"

Blood: "Advance"

Green roll counted.

Callista: "Two just two?"

Night: "Hopefully"

Callista called the porter: "Take their bags."

Room of two's own.

Blood and Night's E-Z phenomenology straw-poll determinate of exactly What the Fuck is Going On at offices of Crack-byte headquarters SCRAMBO.

"We're alchemists"./ boasted.

Data-code-manipulation backdrop: necropolis born of virgin bricks: okay to rebuild precious okay-again. Hiatus not Night: begin the next begin-again soon: eternal clock-tick lurks subjective: watching all you do. Time facts not forever despite vested interest in objective and forever myth-seed illusions of Fate.

Way back Television Days of Daddy-0 Productions: comic sex cartoons: zany characters zany. Imitated The Election: dubbed-over debates. Hilarious voice-overs mocked power-mad fools. Hammed-laughter pissed. Play-Makers confirmed. Play Time Weekly Variety Show — or program or whatever — was da bomb.

Sketch comedies wrote themselves. Monologue codas closed shtick with Happy. Spread the program: embrace Hysterical — and mean it.

Daddy-0 broke 'em up: he kill-destroyed 'em: knocked 'em dead:

"That Daddy-0! He kills me!"

Local theaters clubs bars demonstrate speech of watch-people control: lampoon light but firm: project persona beyond What or Whom.

Money-jokes for bars clubs theaters: hysterical-prophetic when apocalyptic-hip downtown.

Certainly certain someones offered anyone to everyone —

way back Television days.

Blood: "To be young again: alive"

Night: "Too much exhausting now: sleep"

To be certainly certain: like Athena born whole — puked fully clothed and armored from Dad's head.

Night's generation in-of-from gyration hips: shoot location studio: rating season: big indefinite: stay the course: ignore howevers of blind fear: serve to occupy: begin now: live: post-verbal-comic-realism a new comedic form.   Also: effective striving for repaid: steeper: so much television since.

Mommy
can't won't don't
shield you
from
Da Da Dad
Dad Daddy Daddy
Daddy-O
power your plea
cops never wife:
she'll
want
he made
a droolin'
kid

Only way out is in.

How 'bout: "Spend what it takes." And don't request another coffin so damned soon: try not to need one.

"Need a got a hot corn-muffin mister Fat Man...?"

"Call me Daddy-O. Candy?"

Stubby fingers proffered sweets: sweat and chocolate oozed from his plump palm.

Callista described the way-back-when-ago communal Inn Sanity come-go-as-pleased: chill-out.

Before money name change cheap stayed-stilled: a full city block complexed itself: a full city block!

How simple: build a Tech-bar crammed with power gadgets lights and sleek machines: Café Inn Sanity: office-base of Crack-byte: Net-site stuff not magazines: hush-hush.

Us3r tossed kicking and screaming through gates of Academy: degreed: and clinging desperately to Alma Mater's stony skirts. Officially Un-Employed: a programmer seeking labor or (if at all possible) escape.

Us3r to administer the System: Scram the SCRAMBO — and serve coffee upon ./ or Crack-byte team's request.

Life-time regulars and old-timers of Inn Sanity odd-interesting. However: tourists from wherever tourists were-are-possibly-had-been claim they'd been to Inn Sanity — the Original — and honeymooned among aging rich relaxed to live The Day again if ever a day was.

SCRAMBO the world: system planning place: intention of: for something. Emerged lubricated: lost equal shares inherited debt-gain per rough-guesstimate option: closed at one-point-one ennui.

./ said:

Unconcerned. Really: I do not care.

Then there's the matter of dead masters exposed emoting dark-shame afraid-of to the young.

Gloopedy-glooped the System nonetheless. Laughter-music: sex-thunder diffused hard options: processes diverged. Shirt-tie Suits were mimicked: margins of "too-fat too-thin" mocked.

Fuck television: to the pink deeply players of the world!

Happen happened in awkward flame of life (unexpected among 80-year-span Lifers): everyone known known of disappears: decays. No explanation: fade to black.

Night: "The fiction of the fiction: such things exist"

Blood: "Celebrity-Talk-Show Dialog dream"

Night: "My night the same: must be contagious"

Blood: "I'm on-stage"

Night: "Singing. Better songs than god could sing: though god does not sing: god thunders — to be fetched pampered carried adored from one heart-pocket to the next"

Blood: "Everyone loves me: they scream my name"

Night: "I share my sharing personal desires. The host and audience are spell-bound: rapt"

Blood: "Angers: ambitions: everything I'm supposed to"

Night: "With 'the world'"

Blood: "Program the program. Closed loop. Can't escape"

Night: "Nobody escapes?"

Blood: "Nobody cares about worked-their-lives-to-get
cause get ain't worth shit anymore: assuming get
was ever worth getting to begin with"

Night: "Forget get"

Blood: "Forget it: just rage. 'Rage rage against the dying of'
— everything. Rage is all the rage now: it's so raw"

Night: "Wars we imagined ourselves heroes"

Blood: "Shoot and be shot: wounded: save the battalion"

Night: "Callous-cool: smoke-a-lot: laugh at Death"

Blood: "Medal of Honor and maid of honor — just along for
the   bride"

Night: "Home again: disgruntled. Smoke-a-lot-more.
Sunglasses. Tragic-Cool"

Blood: "Narcissism unto necrosis: the works"

Night: "Live for the camera"

Blood: "Our spastic moments"

Night: "Our Network Solipsist. Democracy of tyrants. A
chicken in every pot: a Soap-box on every desktop:
every man a King"

Blood: "Our always ever-more Celebrity Stars"

Yeah yeah yeah: containers of night sear-open burned
sublime: name note of it: brought to you buy caffeine
nicotine: walk drunk the dark city: cover of every magazine:
work a living fiction — your conspicuous puff of do. But still:
nostalgia for breath lingers.

Fear the Future: he's older than Death. Everything felt must
breathe. Flee the phone-call: dance or die: a job awaits!

Resumé: portfolio: thesaurus — find a word for sluggish brain-cells moaning chorus.

Dear Sir or Ma'am:

Fuck off and die. Hate ever again.

Sincerely:

Just Breathe

"Our first real naked" said Blood

"What Life was" said Night

"Gone for real?" asked Blood

"Ridiculous shining. Clown in armor" said Night

"What is it?" asked Blood.

"Ha. Ha" dark Night

"The Pit" cold Blood

"Dance in black?" asked Night

"During the black hours no song. First silence. Same languid bug-eyed barefoot regardless" said Blood

"God creeped-me-out: the whole idea of him" spat Night

"Ugly: horrible: forget it" said Blood

"Return to fit-firm friends not far from young?" asked Night

"Build a dance-floor. In the woods. We'll dance" said Blood

"We'll dance" said Night

Remember me mortal not television horror: he pleaded.

I went yeah: I went yeah yeah yeah.

But antique down-under: nothing left but memories and smoke? *Fuggedaboudit.*

The head barked "Live with me!" as it rolled across the floor.

My slice of years: pointless machines turned Winter to Spring: it's hot. Obvious methods of frustration-torture: bad enough to be crowd-locked in rooms read-write-submitting life-death struggles to Whomever: or school-to-work all day-night-day from cold depression dawn to bleak November dusk. But to be still: anxious: bored: in god-damned fun-love-music weather? Who can work under such conditions? Outrageous. I wanna go out and play. Anyway: how much for the room?

Blood: "Machine for the room"

Us3r: "Rentals plus connection cost"

Blood: "You watch television?"

Us3r: "Try to avoid"

Blood: "You know who"

Us3r: "Of course"

Blood: "Okay then. Machine for the room"

Us3r: "Rentals plus connection cost"

Time passage: minutes: hours: farts in the wind. Of existence.

Night: "Strange kid"

Blood: "Us3r? Just works here"

Night: "Spaced out like"

Blood: "Everyone else just about"

Night: "Must have something going on upstairs you know"

Blood: "SCRAMBO stuff. Computers. Must have"

Night: "Something"

Blood: "Something or other"

Base Operating System SCRAMBO (BOSS).

Us3r administered machines and SCRAMBO Other-detection! (SO!). The Others detected were all code not SCRAMBO hence ripe for decommission and replacement.

Text manipulation pattern port socket zerozerozero — maybe. System performance scramble.

Us3r at Inn Sanity (IS): away from human: delved daily into novel quirks of is: if: and be — conjured by ./ and his techno-somnambulant crew.

Us3r's dull make-money work: paid to look busy: clip-on masks of ardor: do the job cheerful: if possible: if not: with diligence and deep-concern. Do this and They (you know: Them) leave you alone.

Improper speech-gestures and smiles misconstrued render confusion. Avoid sardonic indifference: suicidal boredom: abject despair. And remember: don't do stuff: or if you must do: do as little as possible and badly if not worse: or better yet: worse still.

Regard the situation decently upfront: regardless how criminal.

Clear-safe distance

between

superiors obeyed else *you-don't-wanna-know*

and

customers you show courtesy deference respect — but not
kneel-pucker-up — as you see fit: and again: regard the
situation decently upfront.

I know I know: who to obey?

Depends on Power: how much and how damned ruthless.
And circumstance. The Situation.

Aggression-Power? Or Power protecting profitable? Profitable protects us all from sinister-cunning low-life hustler
evil asshole freak-rat creeps: and thieves.

Power for profit is never evil: ever.

Tomb of the fathers' fathers: your in-heritage of proud what-
why moments sincerely pursued. Didn't dissimulate: like:
"well if not me someone else: no one particular: whoever.
Really any someone-else will do. Don't drive yourself
crazy. Like: whoever..." Through ten: twenty: one-hundred
years in case fright-grief explodes your ticket out this time.
Darkness. Thats your biz — teach me the game too why
doncha?

I'm out of end: no more end for me this time around: I'm
done with end.

Burroughs said: "A paranoid is someone who knows a little
about what's really going on..."

Work directory functions. Check-the-program still a
precious bitch: like Dad. Sad my family: dreamed big about
don't-know-never-been. Bought plug-me boxes: plug-me-
in. Signal-jam this whole damned place if I could — hark! A
wedding song: sung to the tune of "Promise Me" — if anyone
knows it:

oh signal me
through sad-assed fucking places:
I think we need
to make this channel clearer:
better connection:
lock in the mainstream:

(chorus):

access network node
Aaaah-meeeeennnnnn. . .

Us3r refused to be a BadMan.

BadMan: "Never fuck what you wouldn't eat. Haw-haw!"

Woman: "Fag."

Large spread of signs: cheap-print warnings list rules like:

NO LITTERING
NO LOITERING
NO EXPECTORATING free lunch or beer (cause you ain't
gettin' neither)

Just-begin-might-begin might possibly have begun had
things been different: or not: too many signs misread: like
father's terror-eyed recall of ancient train-wrecks lighted
and exposed his core-essentially wrecked *amor fati:* disabled
account: human disambiguate: number: ID: please transcribe.
Thank-you.

"Downright shameful bearing weather-beaten work-day
crosses: *gauche.* We needed colorful costumes: better light-
ing: props: cameras too if possible. Rehearse: perform: capture: set..."

The Deal a perpetual motion machine 24/7: Daddy-O on

top early stayed long. Situations risible: (whimpering street urchins:winter's rag-bundled kids tore everyone apart): always the better option of amuse: away from judgment: promises routine the crowd: Daddy-O's best-biggest: before Night lost her twenty-two forever: succumbed to disembodiment of blue. Before from-the-top rethink. She'd been a talented command-source: so much ahead: so — yawn — detach-resigned: before she lost command:

control:

"Lemme tell you about talk-promises..." Night said.

"The dead guy who monitors Systems said he has a source who lives around here but doesn't go out much cause he talks to ghosts" said Blood.

We unto death:

Blood: "Life on earth: what? Seventy-eighty years? — if you're 'lucky.' Eternity preceded this triple-eternity-to-come accruing interest — already — on time we've wasted wondering 'how the hell when what-for and why?'"

Night: "Fuck your droll epistemology"

Blood: "We'll work it out: you see"

Night: "So many things: can kill you: so many ones"

Blood: "Dog-shit under yer finger-nails. Wash carefully before dinner: plenty hot water frothy lather watch yer step. Remember: one more lawnmower bloody afternoon and no next-morning for you my pretty"

Night: "Serious"

Blood: "Drink while Time"

Night: "Very serious. Where did it all go poof just like that? How? When?"

Blood: "I was eighteen taking a leak against against a tree
one Summer night with Night all hot'n'juicy high as
a kite behind me: zipped my fly: turned around and
— ZAP — here we are."

Night: "Inn Sanity"

Blood: "How we live: center stage didn't choose"

Night: "Doctor lawyer accountant thief: manager salesman
business chief"

Blood: "Eye-magnet: ear drummer: musician: clown. Make
clown-music together"

Night: "Come one come all: see my hear my applaud my
Me: surely you recognize my Name"

Blood: "Shelter a night or two. Here. Inn Sanity. We'll
think: we'll work stuff out"

Night: "Still 'hot-n-juicy?'"

Blood: "Fresh like under the tree and just as nasty. Look:
my fly's unzipped"

Night: "We will we live"

Blood: "We unto Death. Last dance is His"

Sol of our System: Daddy-0 Daddy-0 great uncle egg: nature-
nurture beginning of We: cameras in every room: post-
literate-comic-realism for the celebrity Hoo-Hah set: Sol of
our System light of our Be. Tribal. Patriarch. Four marriages
ten kids three raging ex-wives: and the one who disappeared
— poof — one evening who knows where.

Daddy you promised
we would
promised
we would

promised
promised
promised
we would
be the last.

In this Nation of syndicated time-appointments unfamiliar blood splashed Dead Man's Curve. Questions being reasonable we questioned whether Reason was questionable at all. Convinced others of fleet magic: laughed them to sleep: notorious.

Much is at stake: at night he cried your name.

Bright engine future gleams future of engines: colored prosthetics lack essential sweat of what-do-I-care ability.

For instance: hedgerow scents evoke desire for simple luxuries of Spring. Fear was invented by *dem furriners* (smuggled in from overseas) to tickle misery with gasoline-and-water homilies like "clay can't be helped" on comic talk-show news: a television hoot-virus: virtual but veritable: vapid: vile.

Life goes on: conceal your human-stink like booze-breath: minty-fresh blast: minty minty: freaked-out between the unexpected possible and much-anticipated certain: taller faster stronger smarter: whistle nervously beyond brief-disappointing Past: brief: but disappointing.

Way-back-when Blood cried and cried all through that first cold-shock of school. Haughty: Night rebuked him. She was indifferent to hostile and able to connect dots of crayon-clay construction: her wooden recorder in its corduroy case she carried everywhere — simple free: away — to make heard expressed: back in days of young.

Laughing camera eyes: forest fires: sexy-sultry firm young profit margin: bah sheep shorn: fleeced multitude's notorious

want-more daily. Insipid need-routine: money incites
extreme: bills accumulate: read the papers: dirt cheap talk:
black columns white lies: guns don't kill forest fires drugs
question simple. News-men too: beyond a shadow: doubt
everywhere always at a theater near you: especially here:

where

zealous millionaires partner forever: no *tickee no shirtee*:
nor money-back: forever-day: cash your card no refund
guaranteed: satisfied? Thank you. We appreciate your
business. Come again!

Blood: "I saw the whole race to conclusion of decay:
       humiliation-failure: outrage"

Night: "Not failed just powerless over our own"

Blood: "When we were young"

anywhere always off the well-worn narrative:

Night: "Everyone everywhere always it's too much"

who you are:

"Did Daddy-O have us killed?"

long-faraway-ago:

ghosts in the Machine:

alone in unison to Life each other:

i love you i love you i love you i love you i love you
i love you i love you i love you i love you i love you
i love you i love you i love you i love you i love you.

Prescription states through anxious never-days might mint a new perhaps. Doubtful: muddy ridiculous: afraid of style: won't punctuate unless directed and only when directed if directed: flat-lifeless:

dull:

hurl:

That's all folks.

Exit 40

"Become who you are." — Nietzsche (paraphrased and possibly misrepresented: misinterpreted: bowdlerized and out of context. Hey: like I'd be the first to free-style with his stuff...?)

Back-seat of a speeding limo: Who-To-Become in hot pursuit of Who-You-Are.

High on ridiculous: Become dreamed laughter: applause like incense: terminal notions of hypnotic light: waves of watchers watching.

Become turned (his driver actually: his driver turned) off exit 40 — between the just-begun and ended-all-too-soon — as-always. Still: yet: again.

Drunk on risible: Regard sought antics of Impress: anything on earth to give. What satisfied branch-access of fulfill? Who owned Life: who called Life Home?

Become became uncertain: hence: he conjured Night: droll erotic spider: comic to the core: omnipresent and aloof: gravid with meaning and desire: a necessary phantom. Timing is everything — or nothing.

Night seldom deigned speak to Who-You-Are much less pursue him: she could care less — and usually did.

Night's hauteur aroused Become — almost: never quite actually — to consummate pinnacle of Be.

"Drive limo-man drive!" Become raged buckled — slurping bourbon — tight: determined: in ruthless pursuit of Who-You-Are.

"Relentless" Night sighed and stifled a yawn: "Relentless."

Code-a

Silent is the language of command. The program. Dialect of the machine. The Masters scour data bases with regular expressions honed to pin-point accuracy. Alpha-numeric. Silent hymns to silence. Language without sound. Unless we imagine haunted screams of special characters and typed variables muffled by the disk drive hum — hummmm: hummmmmmmmm — illusion of association snared in skeins of code: open the trope unravel the rope: links to poison applets: you are what you eat — if you can catch it.

I have studied the code and imagined rhythm: meter: lines read aloud: modulated: enlivened by voice: like poetry. As if code could be sung. Or chanted. Life-breath of abstraction: numinous meanderings yanked earthward: matter: sculpted. Elegant rhyme.

$E=Mc2$ in F minor.

The day is near. The coming of Truth as Beauty is at hand.

Time happened. And there was no escape: not even to The Word.

Heart and fraud of the matter ramified: mystified: extended. Circuits. Networks. Clouds. What-have-you.

Bullshit.

I don't ride Their currents.

Say too and Fin's knee.

Au River.

04/23/16 07:11:39 AM

ABOUT THE AUTHOR

Adam Engel . . .

ALSO AVAILABLE FROM
THE OLIVER ARTS & OPEN PRESS

FICTION

THE DECLINE AND FALL OF THE AMERICAN NATION, Novel by Eric Larsen (2013)

THE END OF THE 19TH CENTURY, Novel by Eric Larsen (2012)

THE BLUE RENTAL, Texts by Barbara Mor, (2011)

ABLONG, Novel by Alan Salant (2010)

KIMCHEE DAYS, Novel by Timothy Gatto (2010)

TOPIARY, A Modular Novel by Adam Engel (2009)

NONFICTION

DANCE WITHOUT STEPS, Memoir by Paul Bendix (2012)

THE SKULL OF YORICK, Essays on the Cover-up of 9/11 by Eric Larsen (2011)

AFGHANISTAN: A WINDOW ON THE TRAGEDY, by Alen Silva (2011)

I HOPE MY CORPSE GIVES YOU THE PLAGUE, Essays by Adam Engel (2010)

HOMER FOR REAL: A READING OF THE ILIAD by Eric Larsen (2009)

FROM COMPLICITY TO CONTEMPT, Essays by Timothy Gatto (2009)

POETRY

A CROW'S DREAM, Poetry by Douglas Valentine (2012)

LISTENING TO THE THUNDER, Poems by Helen Tzagoloff (2012)

THE EXPEDITION SETS OUT, Poetry by Alan Salant (2011)

AUTUMN LAMP IN RAIN, Poetry by Han Glassman (2011)

CELLA FANTASTIK, Prose Cartoons by Adam Engel (2011)

Oliver titles are available through any bookseller or at
www.oliveropenpress.com

We hope *[root]* inspires you to look at other Oliver titles.

How did you hear about us? Would you recommend this and/or other Oliver titles to a friend?

Did you purchase this title online, from one of the "usual online dealers," or from the Oliver website?

Did you find this title in a local bookstore?

Please contact us about this book and other Oliver titles you might have read.

Email Oliver's editor and publisher, Eric Larsen:
editor@oliveropenpress.com
or Oliver's associate editor, Adam Engel:
assoceditor@oliveropenpress.com

You can also reach the press by mail:
The Oliver Arts & Open Press
2578 Broadway, Suite #102
New York, New York 10025

CPSIA information can be obtained
at www.ICGtesting.com
Printed in the USA
FFOW03n1125070616
24770FF

9 780988 334373